REDEEMED

a novel

God's richest blessings Donna Dawson!! :)

Donna Dawson

REDEEMED

By Donna Dawson

ISBN: 1-894928-75-X

To contact the author, please email:
authordonnadawson@hotmail.com

Printed by Word Alive Press

WORD ALIVE PRESS

Acnowledgements

To my husband,
who continually supported me in my endeavours.

To my good friend, Wendy,
who pointed me in the right direction.

To my three daughters,
who never let me doubt.

To Sharon, Ciny, Anna and Shelly,
who have cheered me on.

Contents

One

IT WAS NEVER HER INTENTION to become a believer in Christ. She had fallen too far to think she could ever have found her way back to such freedom and forgiveness. God had other plans, though. Will miracles never cease? she reflected as she stared absently through the large plate glass window.

She could see the sun, blood-hued and angry looking, rising over the lake, its silver-grey surface duplicating the fiery disk in its rippling depths. Lake Restoule. It was a beautiful place with its abrupt rocky outcroppings and hills covered with dense collections of brambles, ferns, and scrub trees struggling to maintain their grasp on their barren perches—a place of peace.

She smiled at the glorious sight spread out before her. There was a fine lacy edging of ice skirting the pristine lake water, and the birch, maple and elm trees on the island across from her were absorbing the growing light that was transforming colourless leaves into a blaze of oranges, yellows and bronzes. Early morning fauna were rustling nervously through dry and shrivelled grasses that begged for the approaching rain, and the trees had already begun the slight shuffling dance that precedes a coming storm, their awkward and brittle arms lifting papery foliage in supplication to an overcast sky.

Her focus shifted to the ghostly reflection of her own face mirrored, shadowed and indistinct, in the glass that separated her from nature's canvas, and her smile faded a bit. Her outward appearance was a contrast. Native blood, passed down from her mother, flowed strong in her veins, manifesting itself through the hue of her skin. Long, thick hair bore evidence of her father's Scottish ancestry, it's deep auburn tint muted in the early light. She was a tiny woman, like her mother, slim and willowy with a lithe grace in her movements. Her diminutive size belied an incredible strength of limb. Hers was a body of speed and economy.

Her eyes dropped to the dim reflection of the long ragged scar that traced a wicked path from the corner of her almond-shaped, chocolate-coloured eye to just below her mouth. It was a sad mouth, full and sensuous in shape but with a slight turning down of its corners. It contradicted the peace and joy that shone just below the surface of the rest of her young and lovely face.

But it was her eyes that really told the story. Eyes that had once been full of pain and despair, devoid of hope, now showed slow and steady healing. An unearthly patience, forged in the fires of trial and tribulation, dwelled in their dusky depths, speaking of a life of bitter and harsh experience overcome by great victory. They were ancient eyes.

Chapter One...

Something Is Wrong

HEATHER HAD ADVERTISED A FEISTY NATURE from the moment she drew her first robust breath and followed it with a wail of substantial proportion. Her mother, Jane, insisted her firstborn had received the Mic Mac warrior's blood and the Scotsman's temper, a combination that bore the potency of dynamite. It was immediately apparent that the infant girl was a fighter. She squalled constantly with a vigour that soon exhausted the young mother. From the changing of her diapers amidst flailing limbs and piercingly vocal protests, to the feeding of an unwanted but nutritious food mashed into a disgusting looking goo, the growing tot made a point of asserting her strong will, only backing down when all other choices were exhausted.

*   *   *

Heather's father, Angus MacDonald, seemed to be the only one able to exert a form of control over her that didn't require shattering her stubborn nature. Maybe it was due to the fact that she was a lot like him. He understood the volatile temper and demanding outbursts for what they were—a deep need for much affection and love. He remembered his own mother pulling him onto her ample lap and holding him in an iron embrace until the raging tempest in his own heart subsided. Only then would she talk to him, reprimanding him gently and explaining the reasoning behind her dislike of his particular action. He had incorporated this very method on his own spitfire daughter and marvelled at how quickly she would quiet her tears and yells, look up into his watery blue eyes with her own deep brown ones and touch his coppery beard with a small hand. Her eyes always said what her mouth was unable to say: "I love you"…"Thank you."

Angus relaxed his bear hug with a hesitancy that showed he was not sure that it was safe to do so. She was five and beginning to show some serious strength. This last fit—he had begun to refer to them that way—was far longer and more violent than any he had seen, or, for that matter, any he had thrown as a child. She had graduated from screaming and throwing things to pitching herself on the floor, clawing, and biting at whatever fell into her reach, including herself.

It concerned him more than a little, for although she was tiny of frame, she had a wiry athleticism that could rival the largest of the neighbourhood children. What would happen when she began school in the autumn? Would she be safe from those who targeted the youngest children, bullying them for their own amusement? Would they be safe from her wild and combative tirades? It worried him that Heather had not yet learned to control her temper. On the contrary, the older she got, the worse it became. Perhaps her mother was right about the native/Scottish combination. The thought flickered through his mind like the faint smoke of a single candle. He pushed the brief reflection aside with an inward chuckle. That wouldn't explain the quiet and gentle temperaments —except for the occasional mischievous moment—of the rest of his offspring.

He looked away from his oldest daughter to Charlie and his identical twin George. They were four years old and had neatly divided the personality of one person between them. Charlie was upbeat and easygoing, sporting a sense of humour that, although it led him into trouble sometimes, allowed things to roll off him like water off a duck. He was the doer of the family, pulling toys apart to see how they worked and not worried when he couldn't get them back together. George was quieter, more introspective, and prone to questioning some of his more adventurous sibling's antics. His was the sensitive, artistic nature that enjoyed books and quiet activities. He was the one who often shouldered the responsibility of owning up to whatever mischief the two participated in.

Angus knew Heather's latest fit had something to do with them. It wasn't the first time the dark haired, blue-eyed lads had seen an opportunity to stoke the fires that simmered in their older sister's chest. The two boys had mastered the art of provocation, using it as a form of revenge when their sister overstepped her bounds of authority or became too demanding at play. He had asked them once why they nudged and prodded at her until she could stand no more, and George, in his most serious voice, replied that it was "absolutely amazing" to watch her explode. As much as the response had angered Angus, it amused him that his sons had learned early what his own little sister, Corrie, had used against him in years gone by.

Angus ruminated over what to do with the boys, who now stood guiltily before him. How beautiful they were with their startling blue eyes, the irises rimmed with a fine black line. Hair as black as a raven's wing swirled on their pates, dishevelled from their most recent play. Their skin contradicted them—pale and milky like a bonnie Scottish lass. Ah, but they would be strapping young men when they finished growing, like their father had been.

They weren't bad boys, he knew. Most of the time, the three children played wonderfully together, sharing and laughing and offering to help their mother with little baby Fiona. But then they would grow bored, the meagre toys and books no longer holding their overactive minds, or Heather would become a little too overbearing, bossing and mothering until they had had enough, and the tag team of torment would begin, the boys working flawlessly against her weaknesses, pushing buttons that should be left alone, until she was screaming and throwing things and pounding on them furiously. Had there been only one son, Angus was sure she would have beaten him to a pulp, likely putting an end to it early. But because Heather had to divide her fury, the boys were able to share her wrath, working like two coyotes to take down their next meal, sustaining minimal injuries in the process.

Jane's method was much more down to earth. Since the girl was not to be reasoned with and she became a danger to her brothers and herself, the weary mother would latch a sturdy arm about the child's waist, hoist her to her hip as though carrying a thrashing piglet, mount the stairs that unfolded themselves to the upper story, and dump her unceremoniously upon her bed. Doing an about-face, she would, heart heavy with sadness, slip from the room, empty of all but the bed, lock the solid door behind her, and let her daughter thrash her anger out. It wasn't that Jane didn't care. She cared very much, but with Heather, nothing else worked. No amount of reasoning from her mother could penetrate the wall of noise, anger, and self-absorption that surrounded the child when she had one of her fits, and Jane refused to strike the child in her frustration. Her own life had been filled with enough of that for her to know that there must be other ways to deal with her daughter's problem. One thing was sure—Jane would never permit Heather to act that way without some recourse, and isolation seemed to be the best solution she could think of.

* * *

Angus kissed the top of Heather's head as she slipped quietly from his lap, her tear-smudged face red and puffy and small welts and bruises beginning to appear down her slim arms and legs. She was always filled with shame when the thing was over and would go from destruction to destruction, cleaning and repairing where she could, always hoping to redeem herself, if not to her family, then to herself. She watched her father's eyes grow flinty as they glided over to rest on the two boys shifting nervously from one foot to the other. They cast covert glances back and forth and her gaze narrowed resentfully.

Angus stood slowly to his full height of six feet, his bulky frame towering over the two dark-haired lads. It was time for the young ones to understand what they were doing to their sister and that it was time for it to end. Two meaty work-worn hands descended heavily on identical shoulders and he manoeuvred the boys toward the door that led to the back yard as he spoke.

"We're going for a wee walk, laddies. We have some talking to do."

Jane looked up from her dinner preparations, fighting a small smile as she watched the two drag their feet glumly, marching under the weight of their father's large hands. What would she do without Angus? She shuddered inwardly at the thought of life without him. He was such a good husband and father. Unbidden, her mind drifted back to the events that had shaped the love they shared, and her hands worked mechanically while she dreamed of the past.

*   *   *

Jane never talked much of her own beleaguered childhood. All she had ever really been able to share with Angus was that she had run away from home at sixteen, lied about her age to get a job in a supermarket, and lived for the summer deep in the thick underbrush of the coniferous forest that covered a large part of the province of New Brunswick. It was 1959 when she had chosen the wilderness above her own home's hostilities.

She endured much in that year, saving her meagre wage until she had enough money to rent a small, rundown apartment. She was frugal and fastidious, two traits that had served her well as she had struggled to survive.

During those first three months of freedom, she had bought only basic food each day, soap to keep herself and her few clothes clean, and a good sleeping bag, which she stowed in the hollow of an old tree. She had endured thunderstorms and downpours, cold nights and insect bites. Each morning she rose early and walked from her campsite, concealed with great care within the heart of a copse of evergreens in a denser part of the woods, into the heart of Fredericton. Every penny she earned was funnelled into an account held at a bank not far from her workplace, allowing her to earn the first and last month's rent needed for the apartment essential to survive the upcoming winter.

The apartment was more of a hole underground than anything else, but Jane didn't care. It was snug and the rent was cheap. Standing in the center of the single room, she assessed the sparse furnishings and smiled. In one corner, an old cook stove served as both heating unit and stove. An ancient and worn icebox rested in the other corner. Between the two, like a forlorn and unwanted castaway, sat a small wooden table, thickly layered with paint of different hues, and a mismatched chair.

A cast-iron cot stood against the wall to her left and cradled a moth-eaten mattress of questionable vintage in its rust-speckled arms. This small refuge from the wild and unpredictable east coast elements was nestled under the sturdy stone and timbers of an old cottage at the edge of the fast-growing city, its one flaw being the lack of indoor plumbing. Jane shrugged at that, having grown up without that luxury, and unrolled her sleeping bag, spreading it on the lumpy mattress in preparation for her first night's sleep in her own home.

When the bitter New Brunswick winter crashed down on the city, burying it in a thick blanket of ice and snow, Jane gave in to the need for heat, choosing to use, carefully, her own limited supply of firewood gathered from the same forest she had abandoned that autumn and stored in a small shed nestled against the south side of the cottage. She shared her bounty with the old widow who had kindly rented her the room, and together they fought the hungry and unforgiving season, managing to keep from freezing to death in the generous wind that whipped around the damp stone structure, squeezing itself through the substantial cracks and crevasses that earmarked a neglected building.

She worked diligently at her job, never complaining about her inferior wages or the long hours. Taking as many shifts as was allowed, Jane pushed herself hard, never allowing herself to refuse to do what was asked of her, working her way from cleaning floors and toilets to stocking shelves to working the checkout counter. She ignored the biting cold that nipped at her bare hands and poorly shod feet as she endured the trek to the bank each week to deposit her paycheck, watching with satisfaction as her nest egg grew. It was during her second winter that she met Angus.

At age seven, he and his family had emigrated from the harsh and haunting highlands of Scotland to the small village of Rusagonis, which was nestled within a more south-easterly section of the vast blanket of trees that smothered the province. They had left all they had known of the old world to begin a new life in what was dubbed "the Promised Land." Selling all they had, the frugal family had scraped together enough money to buy passage to Canada, purchase a one-hundred-acre lot, and acquire a dozen head of cattle.

They worked hard, breeding carefully to build up a superior herd, struggling through sheer force of muscle and sweat to increase and maintain an efficient meat-producing operation. For years all went as it was supposed to, and then drought hit. The grain and feed crops withered, providing little with which to sustain their herds.

The following year more than made up for the lack of rain, drowning half the province in a deluge that would rival Noah's flood, and preventing them from planting their fields until well into the short and temperamental summer. The pattern continued for three more years until the price of feed went through the roof, and many farmers were forced to sell off their herds and land. The MacDonalds were, if nothing else, stubborn, refusing to quit, clinging to all they had built with the tenacity of moss to a rock.

Angus was a strapping young man of twenty-one when he realized his father was spending more money to keep the farm running than he was bringing in. After seven years of poor crops the market was flooded with the sale of livestock. As the prices for grain continued to climb, the wages earned at the auction block dropped steeply, bringing less than half the price they would have received a mere decade earlier for a single cattle beast.

He was a giant of a lad with fiery hair that looped and swirled in waves and froths across his brow and down his neck. Freckles were spattered liberally across a slightly crooked nose. His skin was almost milky in its hue, leaving him a target for the sun's most vicious rays. Blue eyes jumped from the tanned and weathered face, pinning down whatever, or whomever they targeted with their intensity. They were eyes that could say so much, one moment twinkling with a merriment that drew the young and old alike, and the next, flashing with a sapphire flame that burned through a person's soul. His face wasn't really attractive, but the eyes—those blue orbs that commanded one's attention with their forceful cast—made him the center of attention within the female population of the close-knit community.

It was his brawn, however, that won him the job at the lumberyard. The young man was six feet of thick bone and heavily fibered muscle. With arms the size of most men's legs, one would think him to be awkward and slow, but Angus had a speed and agility that was surprising for his size. Decades of farming had honed his bulk into a smooth and efficient machine of strength and beauty. Many a day he would work shirtless in the heat, his muscles shifting and rippling with the fluid refinement of a draft horse.

He thoroughly enjoyed the hard work and the companionship of the other men at the lumberyard, absorbing their knowledge and wisdom, sharing in their laughter and harmless pranks. At the end of each day, he would climb into the battered and abused pickup truck and chug his way home, eager and ready for the hearty meal that awaited he and his siblings. Willingly, he poured most of his earnings into the farm accounts, hoping to keep the creditors at bay until the tides turned and the crops were restored to their past bountiful state.

He was not a frivolous young man like others of his age but he did have one small weakness that he made a point to indulge daily. Angus loved red licorice. He stubbornly defended his desire to succumb to the soft and chewy treat, enduring the teasing he received from his coworkers. They were certain that his detour to the local variety store each day had more to do with the young girl, fair of hair and face, who gaped openly at him each time he entered to buy his small confection. Angus, for the most part, hardly noticed her, so impatient was he to make his purchase and return to his job.

And then a day came when the store had no licorice. Someone had missed an order, the young girl explained breathlessly, all the while openly admiring young Angus. Glancing impatiently at his scratched and dirtied watch, the lad turned to leave, unaware of the keen disappointment written on the lass's star-struck face. As he pushed his bulk through the clean glass door, he spied a grocery store further down the bustling street and quickly angled off in that direction, hoping that he could buy his treat and be back to work before his lunch break was over.

* * *

Jane reflected on that first meeting with the man who would become her husband with wry amusement as her nimble hands worked effortlessly at the kitchen sink. She glanced out the window, a dreamy expression still pasted on her face as her mind continued to pull the past from its hidden closets.

*   *   *

She had never been a woman of many words, smiling minimally for her customers as they loaded their various items onto the counter but usually remaining silent. It wasn't that she was rude, but the young native American girl had found it prudent to stay quiet until spoken to so as not to attract attention. She couldn't afford to do or say anything that would jeopardize her job in any way, so she adopted a shy demeanour, striving to blend into her surroundings as best she could.

She didn't look up when the young man placed a package of red licorice on the counter with his massive calloused and tanned hands. But she did notice those hands. She punched in the price and quietly offered him the total, noting abstractly that he hadn't moved to offer the necessary coin.

And then she did look up and her heart stopped. He was a mountain of a man, strong and invincible; a wall of tanned and muscular flesh. He gawked back at her with stunning blue eyes that were flooded with the terror of a trapped animal—and a desire and sudden hunger. Lovely Jane giggled for the first time in her life.

*   *   *

It was much later that Angus told Jane how mesmerized he was by her and how he was forced to stare at the girl like a lost puppy. She was incredibly beautiful, with eyes so dark he felt lost in their depths. Her gleaming black hair fell straight to her waist and was delicately tied back with a deep blue ribbon. She was diminutive, dainty in her movements and actions, and her dusky skin glowed with a warmth that made his toes tingle. She never spoke, but her chuckle was warm and rich, its musical timbre drawing his attention to the fact that he stood there, motionless, holding a package of candy like some great dolt, gaping stupidly at her.

Slowly he put the licorice on the counter and fumbled with his wallet, turning scarlet with his own awkwardness, and when the transaction was completed, he bolted from the store, afraid of what had happened, yet longing to return. His companions knew something of earthshaking proportions had taken place that day, for Angus worked as one in a daze, his mind completely elsewhere. Only he knew that it remained with the exotic beauty who worked at the supermarket a mere five blocks away.

* * *

From that day on, Angus never set foot in the other variety store again. Each day followed the same exciting yet painful routine. He would arrive at work early, push himself hard, glancing occasionally at his watch with a poorly concealed eagerness, and when the time for his break arrived, he would finish the present job, wash his face and hands meticulously and set off for another brief encounter with the woman who haunted his dreams at night and occupied his daylight thoughts.

His fellow workers watched him leave, exchanging sly and knowing looks with one another as he marched off down the street, hair combed into some semblance of order, jaw set, and steely eyes fixed on his target. He would return half an hour later, toss his licorice by his lunch box, untouched, and continue working, distraction dominating his chiselled features.

Jane looked forward to the daily ritual of the giant young man with an eagerness that shocked the reserved woman, and she worked hard to put him at ease, admiring him for his shy and gentle manner. He blushed shamelessly each time she caught him watching her and she lowered her head to hide the secret smile that hovered on her generous lips. Two months it took before he worked up the courage to ask her to come to dinner, and any miniscule thought of politely refusing was squashed when she saw the excited and hopeful expression on his uniquely handsome face.

Jane firmly refused his offer to pick her up at her small and shabby apartment for their Friday evening rendezvous, not wanting him to see the decrepit and decaying building she called home. Her landlady had made it plain that no boys would be entertained in her house—it was not a proper thing for a young lady to do—leaving the young woman with a viable excuse.

Instead, she suggested they meet in the paved lot that lazily stretched itself, grey and pitted, along the full length of the market where she worked. She always finished work at six in the evening and had agreed to meet him there by seven o'clock, giving her plenty of time to change from her work garb into something more presentable.

But what did she have to wear that would make her not look so plain and dowdy? All he had ever seen her in was the generic uniform that all the employees wore. She had never bought clothing for the fun of it and wondered if she should do so before her date.

That Tuesday afternoon, on her way home from work, Jane slipped quietly into the small ladies' clothing store two blocks from her hovel. She had never purchased a dress before and wandered aimlessly down the aisles stuffed with soft and frilly concoctions, reverently touching the odd piece, admiring the soft, feminine feel of it. Suddenly she was startled by the presence of an older woman, stern and stiff, her hair pulled back into a no-nonsense bun, and Jane's hand immediately dropped to her side.

"What may I do for you, miss?" The voice was severe and crisp and Jane cowered inwardly at the authoritarian stature of the woman.

"I…I want to buy a dress. I have a date. I want to look right for it." She spoke quietly, eyeing the rack of more modest coverings that rested against the wall beyond the sales woman. The older lady merely nodded, turning to where Jane's gaze rested and directed her forward with a sweeping gesture.

"I see you have a taste for the more reserved styles unlike so many of your generation. I, too, am more prone to choosing the less revealing pieces." She reached out and pulled a cotton/polyester floral printed dress from the rack and held it professionally against Jane's frame. The young lady gasped at the simple beauty of the three quarter length shift and smiled tentatively into the face of the woman.

"I love it but…how much does it cost? Can I try it on?" Again the voice was quiet—shy—and the elder woman warmed somewhat. Pointing to the change room tucked neatly into the back corner of the crowded room, she nodded in her no-nonsense way.

"You try it on, and I will see what can be done if it is something that suits. I like to encourage today's young people to dress a little more appropriately and if that means I take a little less money, I am willing to do so." She turned the girl and nudged her toward the awaiting closet, dress in hand, and then headed for the cash register to do some figuring.

Jane slipped out of her work clothes and carefully pulled the garment over her head, drawing her thick black braid through the neckline and laying it across her left shoulder. The dress was of a plain cut, showing a hint of her lithe figure without being bold. The neckline scooped slightly, allowing her to wear a trinket while not revealing cleavage. The sleeves, like the skirt, flowed and billowed, starting with a narrow top and ending in a scalloped hem. Muted shades of blues swirled together in fine and indistinct lines, etching out a floral pattern that was subtle and elegant in its composition. She turned and looked at herself in the mirror, stunned at seeing her own image swathed, for the first time, in the luxury of more formal wear. Her perusal was interrupted by the commanding voice of the store's proprietor.

"Well, child, come now and let me see. Hurry up."

Jane scrambled to open the door and stepped nervously from the room. She stood patiently as the woman circled her, devouring every inch of her with a critical eye.

"The length is right, yes. Nothing showing that shouldn't. That is good. But that hair…" She stepped in front of Jane and reached forward, tugging the ribbon from the bottom of the braid. Deftly, the lady ran her fingers through the shimmering silky strands, working efficiently, pulling sections back, twisting and manipulating until Jane's hair sat loosely piled on the crown of her head, the woman's firm hand holding the obedient strands in place.

"There, yes…that's just lovely. That is how you must do it, child." The woman's countenance held no softness and yet, in her actions, she conveyed her approval. And then the woman moved to the side, still holding the thick mane in place but allowing Jane to see her reflection in the full-length mirror. The change was remarkable. With her hair piled on her head, her face looked even more delicate and vulnerable. Her eyes were large with surprise as she admired how the style brought out her high cheekbones and softened the shape of her jaw.

"Go change now and come with me to the front. You must have this dress. It is made for you." She turned and marched her way to the front of the store, while Jane ducked back into the change room and rushed back into her own things, finishing by quickly twisting her long mop back into its nondescript braid.

Later that night, upon reflection, Jane was amazed at how generous the woman had been. She had provided her with a package of straight pins, showing her how to coif her hair properly. The dress had been expensive enough, but undergarments and a dainty necklace had been thrown in to the bargain, leaving Jane with a hefty bundle and a grateful heart. She would make a point of baking the lady some cookies as a way of thanks, no matter how her evening with Angus went. As she meandered the rest of her way home, Jane smiled, determined to become a loyal friend to the kind saleswoman.

* * *

The three remaining days stretched out before Jane mundanely, her only highlights being the purchases of red licorice by an attractive young lumber man. For that small moment of each day, time raced ahead, flaunting and teasing her with a small taste of what was to come that Friday. She practiced the hairstyle each evening, repeating it until it was flawless, each strand of shimmering hair pinned submissively.

Friday came, dragging its heels reluctantly, leaving her distracted and antsy until her fellow cashier pinned her down with a curious glance and a whisper.

"What's with you? You're just a bundle of nerves today. Is it that guy that buys licorice? Are you going to see him this weekend?" The younger girl squealed with delight at the colour rising in Jane's bronze cheeks and she knew her answer without a word being spoken. Her colleague was not exactly close, but they were friendly with each other and Jane merely smiled shyly back at her and winked a glittering dark eye.

Work ended and Jane scrambled home quickly, stopping only once to tap on the department store window and wave at the brusque sales lady. The genteel woman pulled a tight smile and nodded, her eyes twinkling knowingly as she returned the wave with her own royal salute.

In her tidy apartment, she carefully spread out her evening's attire and headed for the bathtub where she scrubbed herself until her skin glowed with health and energy. It took mere minutes to sweep her thick swath of black mane into the elegant hairstyle, pinning it firmly with a well-practiced hand. And then she slipped into the raiment, savouring the transformation from checkout clerk to beautiful woman.

Fashionably late was a term that Jane preferred not to be familiar with, but she had no choice. With all that she had to do, an hour was barely enough to accomplish it all and make it to the parking lot on time. Her heart sank when she arrived to find the lot empty, but then a familiar rumble echoed from around the block and he was there, face flushed and scrubbed clean, wild hair only slightly tamed. She stood awkwardly, waiting for him to park and pull himself from the rusty old truck. And then he walked over to her and suddenly the world was too small for such an extraordinary man. He moved with the confidence that came with his stature, but his face bore the look of a man too stunned to believe what he saw. For the second time that day, Jane blushed.

* * *

Jane cursed as the potato peeler skipped across her knuckle, drawing blood. Quickly, she grabbed a towel and wrapped it tightly around the surface wound. That's what she got for daydreaming like a schoolgirl. She smiled and waited for the blood to stop before resuming her task. She thought back to an admission Angus had made not so long ago. It seemed that he had been just as overwhelmed by her as she had been by him. Her smile widened as the daydream returned.

* * *

Angus was overwhelmed with the intoxicating beauty of the young woman standing alone in the littered parking lot. How could he possibly function with any measure of normalcy with so much distraction to draw his attention from the everyday world around him? She had an uncommon beauty that had only increased with the elegant hairstyle and simple dress. Her eyes were large, fringed with thick black lashes that curled mischievously, inviting him to plunge into the almond depths.

Full, moist lips were parted slightly to reveal large white teeth, slightly crooked, giving her mouth character and definition. Under the soft bronze skin a ruddy tint flooded the high cheekbones. She no longer wore the practical braid that trapped the luscious tendrils of black silk. He openly admired the sweeping strands, blue fire hidden in their depths, as they coiled innocently on her head. She wore a demure dress of blue patterns that swirled and floated about her shapely form, enticing him to look closer, and he swallowed hard, feeling very much out of his element at the moment.

*   *   *

They ate at a small restaurant near the outskirts of the city that claimed to have the best seafood at a reasonable price. While they feasted on the bounty from the Bay of Fundy, they sat and talked quietly of their young lives and their goals and dreams. Jane was adept at steering the conversation away from her own mysterious childhood, always countering a question or comment with one of her own, which drew the topic back to Angus' world, and he was gentleman enough to let it remain that way.

After their small meal, they walked for hours along the less populated streets, enjoying the silences, the soft breeze as it swirled its way through the many buildings, and the sound of each other's voices and thoughts. Jane would not forget the simple comfort and ease of that delightful evening—or the many other evenings that followed it.

*   *   *

Six months after that first date Jane was introduced to Angus' family. His mother hated her. It was plain and simple. Her prejudice couldn't see past the shiny black hair and dark complexion to the beautiful person underneath. His father was more pragmatic. He saw her exotic beauty through male eyes and told his son he understood the attraction but didn't see why he shouldn't stick with his "own kind." It took Jane hours to soothe Angus' wrath. She understood what he didn't. She knew her parents would have reacted the same way in a time where races did not mix. She understood and forgave his parents, knowing it would take hard work, perseverance, and patience to change their minds.

Angus and Jane married a year later in a ceremony that included themselves and the minister and his wife, and began their life together in her shabby apartment with the contentment that only comes to the newly married. In her spare time, Jane slaved at the MacDonald farm, doing any job she was asked to do. Angus was proud of her efforts and watched, amazed, as she won, if not his parents' affection, at least their grudging respect. They worked side by side on the summer weekends bringing in the hay and grain crops, mending fences and shoveling manure, and Jane never once complained, nor did she expect their gratitude.

Weeks became months and her persistence paid off. Through all the hard toil, her gentle manners and giving spirit eroded the barrier of prejudice piece by piece, the final block crumbling when Jane signed over a full paycheck to Mrs. MacDonald to cover a veterinarian bill.

One of their best cows had come down with a severe case of mastitis just after scours had run amok with the spring calves. They had no money and feared having to sell foundation stock when Jane pulled the slip of paper from her wallet and silently handed it to the shocked woman. The elder MacDonald woman dropped her gaze in deep shame as she reached and grasped the paper. And then she rose from the over-stuffed armchair and stood hesitantly before her daughter-in-law. The hug took Jane completely by surprise and she could only respond with a stiff pat on the woman's shoulder.

*　　*　　*

Angus and Jane never knew about the second mortgage or the various loans from people in the community. Not until the stockyard truck pulled up and loaded all his parents' cattle for market did they realize how far in debt the farm had gone. When the 'for sale' sign went up on the front lawn, they knew the inevitable had come and the whole MacDonald family resigned themselves to it.

The farm brought a decent price, purchased by an older doctor who wished to retire and live out his dream of being a country gentleman. Within a month the senior MacDonalds were nicely settled, debt free, in an apartment not far from the small bungalow Angus and Jane shared with their aging landlady.

* * *

How Jane had managed to continue to save was unimaginable, but save she did. They finally had enough money to pack up their meagre belongings and move west to the booming city of London, Ontario, hoping to fare better there than they had in New Brunswick. It didn't take Angus long to find work with a construction company willing to train such a strong and eager lad, and the pay was enough to allow Jane to stay at home with their upcoming child.

* * *

The hiss of burning soup broth brought Jane back from the past abruptly, and she scrambled to remove the pot of boiling liquid from the stove before it overflowed. She resumed her dinner preparations, shaking her head as she watched her husband and sons through the open window that looked out upon the small patch of nature, which embraced the back half of their small house. It was a cluttered bundle of land abundantly filled with foodstuffs and flowers and other growing things. She wondered what he was telling the small boys and how they would react. Absently she shrugged as her mind returned to the setting of the table and her own ponderings.

* * *

Angus seated himself on the rotting stump in the corner of their back garden. It was the one flaw in an otherwise well-tended vegetable patch and he insisted it stay put as his "thinking post," much to his wife's dismay. The two boys stood wide-eyed, shifting restlessly as they waited for whatever punishment was to come. They looked at each other uneasily when their father pointed absently to a patch of grass and ordered them to sit.

"Do you understand why Heather gets so mad, boys?"

Both heads shook from side to side, but their wide and nervous eyes never left their father's face.

"It's like Heather has a little bomb inside of her that she can't control. When you boys antagonize her, it's as though you have just pushed the button to start the bomb. Each time you push that button, the bomb explodes louder and longer and Heather can't stop it." He ran a calloused hand through thinning hair and let out an exasperated sigh.

"Do you understand what I'm trying to say to you?"

Charlie looked at the ground with considerable concentration and then glanced back up at his father.

"Is it like a disease or something?"

Angus laughed, but in the centre of that laugh was a hollow sound echoing the fear of that very thing.

"I don't think so, but it is something she can't seem to help, so don't you think you two should really try hard not to make it worse?"

George turned serious eyes to Charlie and nudged him with an elbow.

"It's like poking a dog with a stick, like you did with Mrs. Crawford's poodle. That's why you got bit, Charlie. Isn't that right, Dad?" He turned innocent eyes back to Angus, unaware of his father's struggle with the comparison between Heather and a tormented dog.

"It's kind of like that, Georgie-boy. Yes. So I want the both of you to promise to keep each other from making Heather mad, just like Mrs. Crawford's poodle. Ok?"

Both dark heads nodded in unison and the three returned to the house with lighter hearts.

* * *

The first unprovoked fit came on a Thursday. It was a cool winter day—the snow had settled heavily on the buildings, trees, and playground—and Heather recalled how it looked as though everything had been blanketed with wet cotton. She was in school enjoying art class. She loved art. She could put her thoughts and feelings into whatever medium was required, emptying her troubled heart and mind of the thing that plagued her. On this particular day she was finger painting. Her paper was filled with bright colours in swirls and flowing designs, bright and full of hope. She was admiring the picture when the strange feeling began.

It always began the same—with a tightness in her chest. And then it felt as though she was instantly shifted to the background of her mind and someone else took over. She was afraid suddenly as she watched her own hands dip into red paint and come out looking as though they were covered with blood. She watched those bloodied hands as from a great distance—watched them recede from her as she drew further and further away from conscious thought.

Later, they would tell her that she screamed through the whole thing. They would ask her why she had struck the girl with the lovely brown hair, covering her with crimson slaps until the girl was laying in a sobbing heap on the classroom floor. They would talk in whispers about how the teacher had to pin her arms to her sides and wrestle her to that same floor until her mother had arrived to take her home. They would look at the bite and claw marks that peppered her lower arms and the bruises that barked along her shins and they would shake their heads in fear, tisking their disapproval. All Heather could remember was that she was in a closet somewhere in the back of her mind and that the other person was doing something with her voice and arms and hands.

Upon arriving home, she climbed the abundance of stairs, dragged herself into her barren bedroom, and collapsed on her bed, sleeping deeply for three long hours. Her father's voice, heavy with worry and anxiety, slowly drifted to her, subliminally urging her from her stasis. Her drowsy eyes fluttered open, drunk with the after-effects of her earlier violence. It took moments for the pupils to focus, pushing aside the murkiness to unveil the shocking view of her parents pressed in close, fear mingling with the tears that filled their worried eyes.

"Wake up my wee lass. You've been asleep far too long."

His voice was quiet like a soft spring breeze and Angus stroked her hair gently with hands stained and calloused by many hours of hard labour. She sat up with effort, her head cottony, and they talked about what had taken place. With each syllable that wriggled its way into her weary mind, with each word that formed the sentences that described her wretched actions, Heather became more disheartened and filled with shame. Her parents reassured her of their love, comforting their daughter as best they could, and while she sobbed uncontrollably against her father's flannel covered chest, she failed to see the look of frustration and uncertainty that passed between them. For the first time since the birth of their oldest daughter, Angus and Jane knew something was drastically wrong.

Two

HEATHER OPENED THE WINDOW that barred her from the crisp northern air and breathed deeply. It was always a painful thing to remember her early childhood. And yet it was the time that held some of the sweetest memories.

For every fit of evil temper she displayed there were a dozen fleeting moments of blissful play with her siblings and her parents. Even now, images of Charlie and George, short legs pumping furiously as they ran wildly in a game of tag with her while Fiona stood by, thumb firmly planted in a puckered mouth, flooded across her mind's movie screen.

Absently, she stroked the angry scar on her cheek as she called up more of the play times prior to her school years…taking turns pushing Fiona on the swing…fishing in the small creek that ran through the orderly park four blocks from their home…baking cookies with her mother so she could play dress-up and tea time with the younger ones. She had loved her family fiercely and hated what she had become when the anger came upon her. It was an ugly stain that blighted the joy and laughter they had shared.

Suddenly the young woman felt claustrophobic and turned abruptly to the door. No one stopped her, nor was there need to question her destination. That was part of who and what Heather had become. She would grow silent and stare off into the distance and then, like a trapped rabbit, she would become subtly agitated, stroking the poorly healed wound on her face. It wasn't long before she was striding off into the open air to stand by the edge of the lake, drawing strength from the Master Creator by immersing herself in His creation.

The remembering was painful…and cleansing. It wasn't Heather's first time sifting through the archives of her young life, but each time she did it, it was therapeutic, purging one more file, clarifying and healing one more detail.

She glanced into the water. The scar—again. Each time she saw it, she would remember. Each time she remembered, it would be easier. Each time God would step in with the cleansing spirit she badly needed.

Chapter Two...

Violence Comes

HER FOURTEENTH BIRTHDAY HAD COME and gone without incident. Heather breathed easier knowing it had been a happy time for all concerned. She couldn't help but feel the tension that clouded the happiness of the day. They all wondered if it would happen again. They all feared that it would and the day would be ruined no matter how hard they tried to pick up the pieces after.

It frightened the young teen to think of some of the things she had done during each of her fits, and every one of them widened the gulf between her and her family. They loved her, she knew, but between them a distance was growing. They were uncertain around her—afraid. And who could blame them?

Her guests, few as they were, were gone, and she drifted through the house sombrely, no longer needing to plaster the fake smile on for the benefit of those around her. She lingered in the family room doorway, abstractly scanning the room, not knowing what she sought, and then her eyes rested on the mantel where the photos were displayed proudly. She meandered over to them, as though drawn by some unseen string, and stopped before each one, devouring every detail so as to permanently imprint them in her brain.

Heather gazed longingly at the latest family portrait photo. It was a beautiful picture. A perfect picture. A lie. Everyone involved with their family knew that life was difficult in that household and it all pointed to Heather's fits. There had been doctors aplenty. Psychiatrists. Social workers. Useless medications. Even a psychic was called once and upon meeting Heather, shook her head fearfully and left. Her sigh was filled with all the longings since time began and she traced a finger over each family member's face.

Her father's hair was thinner than ever but still gleamed with the same bronze tint her own locks contained. His eyes crinkled, but, yes, there it was—that edge of doubt and fear that never left after the first attack on her schoolmate. Her mother's hair was greying fast but she still carried the beauty that had drawn Angus to her. Her smile was tired…a worn smile.

Heather's finger drifted to her twin brothers. If you didn't know better, you would think they were older than her the way they protected her. Even in the photo, they hovered, leaning toward her, the angles of their bodies appearing to shield her slightly. She focused her attention on her own face smiling back through the camera lens and she shuddered a little. The eyes didn't really seem like her eyes. They were the right colour—that chocolaty hue that devoured the pupils—but there was an otherworldliness about them, a slightly crazed look…and behind that, a poorly masked glint of panic. She recalled having a fit not long after the camera shutter clicked, and in her violence, she almost destroyed the photographer's studio. She clearly recalled the humiliation of offering to clean up and being soundly yelled at by the terrorized man.

And then there was Fee…Fiona…beautiful, shy, gentle Fee. She sat away from Heather as though it wasn't quite safe to be close. It wasn't. Her dark mousy hair and hazel brown eyes housed within them a freer, lighter spirit, filled with sunshine and the sweet fragrances that drift on fairy winds from the craggy rocks of the highlands. It was as though the picture portrayed the true story. Where Heather was total darkness, Fiona was bright fire and shining light.

Heather adored her little sister with a fierceness that left no room for jealousy or sibling rivalry…and feared for her with that same ferocity. The fits, vicious and tempestuous, were, of late, targeted toward the youngest MacDonald child as though somewhere deep inside of her, a part of Heather wanted to eradicate the beauty and purity that was her little sister. Heather's heart constricted with indescribable anguish to think that she was so single-mindedly capable of destroying such a sweet soul.

Fee, for her part, forgave, gently approaching her sister to stroke and massage the guilt from Heather's tear-stained face. It was a contradiction as old as night and day. One minute, a railing she-demon was thrashing and flailing against reinforced walls, Fee huddling terrified at the end of the hall listening to the obscenities spewed at her. Then silence would come, followed by the soft weeping and whispered repentances, and the youngest child would creep to the door, let herself in and quietly soothe Heather.

Heather knew. There would come a day when the creature in her would outwit them all, and Fee would suffer for their inadequacies. From that dark and festering thought came the barest whispers of a plan. She must leave. She knew most children ran away because they wanted their own way or wanted to punish their parents. Some ran because life was a horror, filled with abuse and unspeakable torments. She was sure she must be the first teen to run away in order to save her family.

She turned the gilt-framed photo face down and slowly walked from the living room to the stairs that led up to her bedroom, her heart heavy from the guilt and shame of who she was. She stood in the doorway and surveyed all before her with weary eyes. The room was bare, all but for her bed. The window was boarded shut and the door was furnished with a sturdy deadbolt. She cringed at the claw marks on the walls and the cracked drywall where she had thrown herself in every direction. Some scratchings were old, others recent. Her father had long since given up repairing the plaster and paint, for no sooner would a fresh coat dry, and she would shred it with her cracked and broken fingernails.

Her bed was neatly made and rested in the centre of the room. That was her way of showing her family she tried. When her fits were over, she would calmly and meticulously straighten the bed, dragging the mattress back to its proper place, and drawing the sheets and blankets over its battered shell. She would proceed around the room, surveying the damage with a heavy heart, looking for new cracks in the wall or fresh bite marks or tears in her bedding. And when she had finished all she could do, she would return to the bed and sit and wait for the silence to inform her family that it was over while tears of remorse and defeat beat tracks down the soft skin of her dainty face.

She was grateful for one small mercy. She could still feel a fit coming and would quickly head for the stairs. No one needed to say anything. Everyone knew and someone would always follow at a distance to lock the door.

* * *

Heather knew, even as she felt the fit taking hold, that Fee would be the one to follow her to her room that day. All afternoon she could sense the restlessness of the thing and yet it held back…waiting. In retrospect, she probably should have just gone to her room and stayed there. But she hadn't and the creature was patient, waiting until the others were too occupied to interfere. And then it came to her suddenly, giving her scant time to scramble up the stairs to the safety of her prison. She could feel it writhing within her, clawing its way forward, whispering obscene things to her, laughing at her and telling her—Fiona is coming this time.

Fiona wasn't prepared for the super strength that poured itself upon her through the hands and teeth of her sister. She had kept back like she had been told to do, but Heather had tricked her. She had watched her sister stagger up the stairs as quickly as she could and had seen her enter the room. She didn't know that she waited just beyond the door, and when Fee reached the stair landing, she was astonished at the speed and force with which her older sister hurled herself upon her, knocking her to the floor with a loud crashing of pine boards.

She barely had time to let out her own screech of fear before it was drowned out by the howling and ranting of her demonic sister. Fingers that, moments before, had softly stroked the keys of the battered piano, were now curled into claws that slipped eagerly about the youngest child's throat. The maniacal laugh increased with the pressure of the squeezing as the thing in Heather attempted to compress the soft tissue in Fiona's neck. She struggled back in a desperate attempt to draw in much-needed air, clawing uselessly at the vice-like grip and flailing wildly with her legs, each kick weakening as her oxygen supply diminished.

She was nearly unconscious by the time her father came stampeding to the rescue, taking the stairs two and three at a time. He grabbed Heather by the collar, desperately shaking her, hoping to loosen her grasp. In one last effort, the giant gripped his daughter's hands with his own powerful hold and forcefully pried them from Fiona's battered neck. The poor girl lay there, hungrily gulping in great mouthfuls of air, and watched as her father dragged Heather's thrashing, violent body into the room. It was all he could do to keep her there and close the door at the same time. Fiona laid there, her last impression being the look of hatred in her sister's eyes as she glared over their father's shoulder at her. Spittle flew from Heather's mouth as she heaved one final string of curses before the door slammed and the lock clicked, and then Fiona's tears came, enveloped in heaving sobs. She sat, cradled in her father's tender arms, crying out her anguish over a sister who loved her—who hated her.

The bruises appeared the next day—huge, ugly, deep purple welts. Heather was stunned at the finger imprints on her little sister's neck and the fat lip that had swelled the night before. Dark purple shadows spattered themselves liberally down small arms and legs where Fiona had been flung angrily to the floor. Heather knew it was her own handiwork and immediately fled to the bathroom, throwing up repeatedly. Once she had retched until she could retch no more, she rose from the tile floor, wiped her face with cold water, and nodded resolutely to her reflection. It was time.

* * *

The walk to the bus stop was silent, Heather trailing resolutely behind her two brothers and sister. She watched them carefully, sensitive to the distance they allowed her to keep, wishing it didn't have to be there. She waited until the bus was almost at the bus stop when she called to her siblings.

"I won't be going to school today."

The three looked at her warily and she repeated it.

"I won't be going to school today 'cause I'm leaving home."

It wasn't sinking in.

"I've hurt this family enough and it's got to stop. No doctors have been able to do anything and Mom and Dad can't protect you guys much longer. I love you but I've got to go. You can't say anything. You all know it's the right thing to do."

Fiona was sniffing and wiping tears. Heather gently wiped Fee's tear, touched the bruise on her mouth and hugged her, and then she turned to her brothers, handing them a forged note in a sealed envelope.

"Give this to my teacher so they won't call home. Look after Fee for me, will ya?" Quickly, she threw an arm around each lad, squeezed briefly, and turned away as the bus rounded the block. Ducking into a row of lilac shrubs, Heather was gone before the bus driver could see her.

She had planned well and pulled a change of clothes from her pack. She knew she could disappear in a big city like Toronto much easier than in smaller London, so she headed east. She had studied maps of Ontario and decided her best course was to travel at night and follow the 401 Highway.

Her heart was heavy with the knowledge that she might never see her family again, but she knew this was the right thing to do. In the time since she had first conceived the idea to run, Heather had read numerous survival books, taking weekly trips to the library and furtively collecting the supplies she would need. Once, her mother asked her about her interest in the library, wondering if there was a boy involved. Heather had laughed, working hard to put light heartedness into it, and told her mother that she had a project to do at school and needed to do research for it.

Threading her way through familiar streets, Heather kept a nervous eye on the traffic and the people around her. It was obvious that she should be in school, but she clung to the hope that none of those who passed her, absorbed in their own busy lives, would take notice of one truant teenage girl.

Keeping to the shadows and alleys of the tidy mid-sized city, Heather avoided scrutiny, ducking into malls or shops to avoid patrolling police or curious stares. Eventually, she wound her way to Highbury Avenue where it met the 401 Highway, relieved to see her first goal in site. Walking brusquely, she waited until she was outside the city before trying to hide her trail.

The drainage ditch that she slipped into was full of cold and brackish water and Heather cringed as she began to thread her way along the edge of the highway. Dozens of cars and trucks zipped past her on the four-lane expressway, but no one paid attention to the young teen, running, shoes in hand, wading aimlessly through the marshy ditch, the razor grass and bulrushes dragging at her pant legs and scraping her ankles raw. She trekked along at a steady pace for a couple of hours, noting that her feet were getting quite wrinkled, before she started scanning the tree line for a good place to duck for cover. She had passed a few farms and was looking for a thick woody area to slip into, noting that the foliage was getting denser with each passing mile.

Finally, Heather spied an opening in the woven wire fence that seemed to accommodate a deer path and she removed her backpack quickly. Keeping a cautious eye on the traffic, her hand groped for the large bag of black pepper. She sighed as she pulled it free of the pack's confines and tore a small hole in the bottom. Patiently, she waited for the gap in traffic that she knew would come and then scrambled backwards toward the fence, sprinkling the pepper liberally over her tracks like the survival book had recommended. The book had stated that it was a great way of throwing predatory animals off of her trail, but it could also make them angry as it burned their noses.

Heather hoped they wouldn't send tracking dogs after her, but if they did, she wanted to be certain they wouldn't find her trail. She prayed to unknown gods that, if dogs were brought out, none would turn on their handlers. She pushed the thought aside and continued backwards, stumbling over twigs and rocks buried beneath the long grass that had been knocked flat by an earlier storm, until she pushed herself, rump first, through the gap in the fence. Right then, survival and escape were all she must focus on.

The pepper lasted for a good distance and when the last grains finally trickled through the torn plastic, Heather stuffed the empty bag in her pocket, sat on a nearby stump, and donned her socks and runners. She took a last, longing look in the direction of home, turned, and sprinted down the path, careful to watch for hidden obstacles that might snag her or pull her down.

She continued at a steady pace for as long as her lungs would permit, always keeping the highway within sight to her right through the thicket. She hoped the police would assume she had gotten a ride heading west, since she had come to the north side of the highway, but she couldn't take that chance. Her best ally was distance and she was determined to put as much of it between herself and her family as she possibly could. At least Charlie, George, and Fiona wouldn't tell on her. She was certain of that. She had until three-thirty that afternoon to get as far as she could before finding a secure hiding place, and then she would have to wait for dark to resume her journey into the unknown.

Time ceased as Heather trudged on. The sun rode high in the sky, throwing a piercing heat down on her. She estimated that she had traveled fifteen miles. That left her with another eighty-five or ninety miles to go. Checking her watch, given to her the Christmas before, she eased herself down a slope that led to a culvert under the highway, noting that she had gone beyond the time limit she had set for herself. Working her way along the edge, she figured she'd be able to stop there without being seen. If she grabbed a couple of hours of sleep, she'd maybe get another twenty or twenty five miles in before morning. Leaning back against the cold, rounded steel, Heather propped her pack behind her head, closed her eyes, and dozed.

It was dark when she woke and Heather checked her watch quickly, a small panic rising in her chest. By the slight moonlight she could just barely see that it was ten-thirty, and she let out a sigh of relief. Stepping out of the storm drain, she turned her head both ways, stretching out the kinks and letting her senses adapt to the dark that draped like a heavy veil around her. The traffic was steady on the four-lane highway above and to her right, leaving her no choice but to continue following the ditch beside the road. That meant wet running shoes, but she could let them dry in the morning. She started out slowly, allowing her pupils to expand enough to permit the insignificant moonlight to illuminate the boggy, obstacle-ridden trail. Within moments she was able to define shapes, and numerous shades of darkness gradually separated themselves into the shadows of shrub and grass.

She traveled late into the night, slogging endlessly in the swamp that ran parallel to the road above her. Eventually the traffic ceased and Heather knew it was well past midnight. Doggedly, she dragged herself out of the ditch and onto the gravel that lined the sides of the 401. It made for much easier walking and she hoped to gain some time.

She pulled an energy bar from the pack and chewed as she walked, her feet blistered and raw from the friction of her wet socks and shoes. Her heart was numb. Would her parents still be awake or would they sleep better knowing their other children were safe from her? It was an uneasy question that she really didn't want an answer to. She hoped the police wouldn't start a search until morning. It was unlikely they would, leaving it safe for her to be so close to the road, but after her first night away, everything would be different.

A tear trickled down her olive-coloured skin, etching a track through the smudges of dirt and grime. She ignored it as she picked up the pace. Self-pity wouldn't help her, nor would thinking about her family. She had done what she had done for their sakes and it was time to press on.

* * *

In the east, a faint glow eased its way onto the horizon, telling Heather that it was time to hide. She was bone weary, ready for tears again, and almost willing to flag down the next vehicle heading west toward London. And then she saw Fiona's fearful face accusing her for her violence. Setting her jaw, she strained her eyes forward into the distance, hoping to see another culvert, but all she could see were shadows and the headlights of an oncoming vehicle. She quickly stumbled back down into the ditch and crouched, hoping the oncoming vehicle wouldn't see her. The familiar roar of a transport truck increased as it thundered past the spot where she had stood not moments earlier. She waited for the rumbling whine of the diesel engine to fade into the distance and then Heather, adrenaline pumping, began to run, hoping to find something before the next vehicle arrived.

In this way, she spent the next hour, dodging traffic, searching desperately for a place to hide. She had just hunched down to wait out the next string of traffic when she spied the telltale signs of the next storm culvert. In the distance, she could make out the edge of corrugated steel glinting dully in the early dawn. She waited, breathing heavily, until she could no longer hear traffic, and then she was up and running hard, her eyes fixed on her target with a bold determination.

Although it felt like hours, it only took a few minutes for Heather to slide into the culvert. Her timing was perfect as she heard the dull thumping of another transport passing by overhead. She drew in air with loud gasps and wormed her way further into the drain. Much to her relief, it sat higher than the murky ditch and was dry. Only a minimal amount of debris littered the tunnel that ran the full width of the highway above and she was quite proud of her find.

She removed her wet shoes, laying them and her socks near the edge to dry. Unconsciously, she quickly threw a glance to her left and right before slithering out of her mud-and-slime-stained pants. Too cautious to leave them with her shoes, she fumbled her way back to the spot where she had left her pack and tossed the pants in a heap a few feet away, hoping they would dry enough before the next night-trek she would face. Slipping on the only other pants she had brought, Heather stretched out on the hard packed dirt, closed her eyes, and slept soundly.

The loud rumble of her empty stomach roused Heather from her deep sleep and she sat up groggily, disoriented in the darkening storm drain. As her mind adjusted to the foreign environs, she rose, crept to the edge of the culvert, and surveyed the surrounding territory cautiously. Wanting to silence the persistent growl in her lower parts, Heather rummaged deep in her pack, pulling out another power bar to munch while she planned the coming night's strategy. She gulped a long swig from her water bottle and tested her shoes for dryness, slipping on the stiff, gritty socks first.

She had slept the whole day away and knew by the quickly fading light that it was time to move on. Another night would hopefully see her in the big city. She had even planned that out. In her naivety, Heather had assumed she could find work. She would, like her mother, survive on little.

The air had cooled somewhat with the approach of night. Heather sniffed the slight breeze that teased about her, as though to smell for possible danger. Her amateurish senses could only detect the damp mustiness that precedes an October rain. Somewhere to her left, in the tree line, she could see the faint outline of a young deer, its head raised, and ears cocked forward. Upon seeing her, the fragile looking animal bunched its lean muscles and bounded back into the bush from whence it came, the rustling and crashing of foliage its only evidence of having been there. It was almost as though the good creature could feel the presence of the evil monster that was, once again, grappling its way into the core of Heather's soul.

The girl tensed as the feeling snaked its way through the various channels of her mind, beginning, again, its litany of her faults and imperfections. Hurriedly, she pitched her backpack down toward the ditch and then crawled back into the center of the culvert as the fit took hold. She thrashed and screamed, slammed her fists on the dirt floor and pulled her hair. She was loud and ferocious within the culvert's confines—and oblivious to it all until it was finished. And then, as always, she slept hard.

Heather awoke in the dark again and struggled once more to reorient herself. It took some time to find her pack as there was so little light from the thin sliver of moon that peeked now and then from behind the murky clouds. Fortunately, she had aimed well in her frantic state and it had caught and held on the sturdy branch of a soft maple tree. It took her forty aggravating minutes to loosen it from the tangled grip of the twigs that ran the length of the slate-coloured branch. She yanked tenaciously until it finally gave way and she tumbled backward onto the damp grass, pack in hand. Shrugging into the shoulder straps, she strode angrily toward the city, ignoring the fine drizzle that had begun falling gently about her. She might have been there already had it not been for her fit.

For the first time since she had left home, Heather experienced some of the difficulties that a runaway must face. The increasing rain cooled the air until she was forced to pull out her windbreaker and one of two sweaters. By the time she found sufficient shelter, her hair was soaked and plastered to her head in long ropey strands. Water trickled steadily down her back, causing her to shiver violently from time to time, and she could feel her skin pucker and wrinkle from the constant contact with waterlogged clothing. Her shoes squished and sloshed, needing to be emptied every so often. She was certain her lips were blue and she could only hope that her matches were dry enough to start a small fire to stay warm. Just as the black of night began to bleed into the grays and muted greens of early dawn, the rain stopped and the air began to warm a little, leaving Heather hungering for the scant heat it provided, all the while wary of the encroaching daylight.

She was grateful for the people who had planned and constructed the highway with such care and precision. Because of their foresight, an abundance of culverts could be found. She was desperate to retreat deep into the heart of the next one, hoping to find enough debris and garbage to burn. She just hoped no one would notice the small waft of smoke making its way through the opening in the ditch. That would cause a stir.

* * *

It was amazing how much bark, twigs, scraps of paper and plastic collected along the sides of a storm drain. A small trickle of water meandered slowly along the bottom of the curved metal tunnel, but other than that, the drain was dry. A small fire crackled merrily, producing little smoke. Heather had plenty of dry kindling to keep the fire alive and hot, and it wasn't long before her fingers lost their numbness and her clothing began to steam.

She was thirsty, having emptied her water bottle hours before, but didn't trust the runoff water. Her survival book suggested boiling the water for seven to ten minutes before attempting to drink it, but she was too cautious for even that. She wanted to know the source first. Climbing to her feet, she followed the stream back to the south side of the highway and carefully glanced out into the bright daylight, eyes straining to follow it further. The girl was pleasantly surprised to see a marshy spot in the ground, water bubbling musically from its center.

This ditch was higher than the north ditch, leaving it dry, all but for the small spring. From what Heather could see, the water ran through the culvert to gather in a stagnant, murky pool that ran the length of the ditch. She groaned with disgust. All that time, she had walked in marsh and swamp when she could have walked on solid ground. Well, at least she hadn't left a traceable trail.

She cast a glance about her, looking for something to withstand the heat of her cheery fire and her gaze landed on a large tin can. Half the label was gone but she recognized a brand of canned peaches from the store. It was half filled with mud and silt but it was without holes. Eagerly, she pulled it from the muck, rinsed it thoroughly in the fine trickle of water, and returned to the spring. Her ears had become slightly more acute in the past two days due to her heightened level of nervousness, and she waited until she could hear no traffic before scampering into the sunshine to collect her water. Twice, she had to abandon her small container at the spring, ducking back into the culvert before a passing vehicle could notice her, but finally the tin was full and she carefully set it on the ground by her fire.

It took some time for her to build the tiny blaze back up and to find a suitable flat rock to set in its center, but eventually she sat back, waiting while the water steamed and hissed from its canister nestled in the heart of the licking flames. She dozed briefly, her thirst keeping her from the sound sleep she needed. Through drowsy eyes she watched as the water surface smoked and misted over and then transformed into the rolling boil. She glanced occasionally at her watch, timing the seductive brew, and when it was ready, she pushed the coals and crackling sticks to the side, forming a separate fire further away and leaving the charred rock alone with the tin perched atop.

Heather had never tasted water so sweet as she did that day, and she gulped the still warm nectar greedily. Several times she repeated the process, drinking more and filling her large bottle until it brimmed over. Tamping out the fire, she settled down for yet another day's sleep, knowing that the next day would see her in the big city. Not for the first time, a nervous flutter tweaked her stomach muscles at that overwhelming thought.

Three

HEATHER SMILED SADLY AT THE FLOOD of early memories. She had been so naïve then. She tossed a pebble absently into the water. So many years had been wasted when all along the answer hadn't been too far from her. Pushing the thought away, she breathed deeply and began to stroll along the peaceful shoreline.

Still looking out over the beautiful lake, she was unaware of the beautiful panorama. The mallard duck family that swilled its way through the heart-shaped water lilies not twenty feet from her went unnoticed. Neither did she hear the call, echoing hauntingly over the water's surface, of the cow moose on the other side of the lake or the bull's deep and resonant answer. She was too absorbed with the looking inward to enjoy what was around her.

A loon piped its mournful song as though reading Heather's thoughts. Even nature understood what it was to suffer greatly. And then silence drifted across the lake, interrupted by the occasional chirrup of the last of autumn's frogs as they floated in the reeds.

Heather allowed her mind—forced her mind—to finish that first journey. She tasted each detail as though to be certain no ingredient was missed. She could still feel the damp grass on her blistered feet as she had walked her third night away. She remembered, clearly, the shock of discovering how quickly country transformed to huge city as she approached the outskirts of Toronto.

Chapter Three…

The Scattered People

HEATHER SPENT THAT LAST DAY of her road trip sleeping in a dense clump of sumac bushes overlaid with a tenacious and abundant wild grape vine. It had made the perfect tent, allowing little light to touch the soft ground around the collection of roots, keeping her invisible to any passers-by. She even enjoyed the small, sweet grapes clustered deep within the heart of the vine, eating her fill of the dark and shrivelling fruit.

Autumn had been a pleasant surprise that year, gifting the southern part of Ontario with unusually warm weather. Frost hadn't come yet, nor had the leaves, painted in yellows, reds and oranges, left their summer homes in the trees to migrate to the ground, forming a blanket that would protect the grass from the winter's ravages.

Heather hadn't anticipated the warmth but was grateful for it for the most part. She had slept lightly that day, feeling the bite of small insects and the closeness of the air, and when night called around, she waited until it had cloaked the city in its thickest garment of black before she crawled from her safe place to finish what she had begun.

She swallowed her first taste of real fear as she slipped furtively past vagrants and drunks, avoiding their accusing and suspicious glares. She wandered aimlessly, like they, until she found a large park nestled on the edge of the city's working district.

The park was the community's attempt to bring as much wilderness to the city as was safe to do. It boasted huge and aged trees of different varieties and lilac shrubs left to sprawl in great clumps. Sumac, with its ever-present companion, the wild grape vine, filled in small gullies and rock-strewn knolls, and in the open areas well-groomed gardens dotted the neatly clipped grass. A narrow sidewalk wended its way in various directions through the entire common, giving the daytime citizenry a relatively safe pathway from which to view the various flora and fauna within the broad borders.

Those who walked the city's night streets found nooks and crannies within the shelter of the park's foliage to sleep the day away. The more upright residents of Toronto seldom left the footpath for fear they would find and awaken that part of society which most chose to ignore. Some of the vagrants wandered through the park during the lunch hour, hoping to touch the heartstrings of the working class enough to receive coinage to feed their addictions or food to fill aching bellies, but for the most part, both classes were content to avoid one another.

Heather was relieved to find such a haven of wilderness in the city, for this was something she was now familiar with. Her unkempt appearance had thrown her in with the rank and file she had heard her parents refer to as street people. Her disguise was so complete that she was left unmolested as she nervously shimmied up a large walnut tree and quietly watched the grounds below, making little sound as she harvested and awkwardly shucked a small amount of the ripe nuts that grew in abundance in the branches around her.

She was left alone those first few days. That was a bigger miracle then she knew at the time. Her pack carried only her water bottle, which she filled from the drinking fountain near the public restrooms, the survival book, her small collection of clothing, and a small Swiss army knife with which she pried the hard shells from her only source of nutrient.

Heather felt the frustration of rejection after rejection as she tramped the busy streets looking for a job. The days of hiring without questions were gone and no one was willing to take a risk with the teen. Had her isolation continued much longer, the girl might have given in, begged a quarter, and phoned her parents to come pick her up. It was not to be.

The first frost hit the city with a vengeance. Grass that had leapt forth with an emerald vibrancy the day before, now lay heavy and dull under a blanket of crisp, white crystals. Cars and trucks no longer zipped by with windows wide open in carefree abandon. They crept along the darkened roads with caution, closed up and huddled against the bite in the air.

Heather had solved the problem of food five days after arriving in the park. It was amazing how wasteful people were, and Heather had become so hungry that she tossed her inhibitions to the wind, stooping to sift through the several garbage cans dotting the pathway that cut through the park. She tried her hand at begging and was soon shocked at how uncaring people were. No one wanted to feed a helpless waif, let alone acknowledge that she even existed.

She had taken full advantage of the dingy public washroom, ignoring the filth-stained walls while she struggled to maintain a level of cleanliness that might make her acceptable to any potential employer. Her stomach growled constantly as her search for food became her main priority, and her life became a cycle of walking and sleeping by day and perching in a tree by night so as to survive the urban wild.

* * *

She shivered. Her lips were blue from the cold. How she had survived through the freezing night, she would never know. Like each night before, she had shimmied up the same walnut tree, wedging herself into the crotch where three large branches shot off into different directions as though searching for some quality of nature in the midst of city. All went as usual until the thermometer dipped so low that she couldn't keep warm. Her teeth chattered noisily and she might have frozen to death if she hadn't decided to turn around, putting her back to the slight breeze. In doing so, she noticed the light through the spaces in the branches and watched as, one by one, the street people left the park, drawn to it.

* * *

Heather hesitated only briefly and then, with a last shiver, dropped from her rustic haven down to the crisp grass, creeping carefully toward the flickering shadows dancing temptingly on the brick wall in the alley across from the park. It was her first experience with the wary camaraderie of the harmless vagrants and she huddled just behind a half dozen others of various ages as they stood around the scant warmth of the fire.

It was fed with garbage and cast-off furniture and it smoked and popped, merrily, in the metal fifty-gallon barrel. Her only thought, beyond keeping from being discovered, was to steal a small share of the heat escaping past the foul-smelling bodies that jealously guarded the flames.

For hours she had stood, saying nothing, keeping to the shadows, hording what heat drifted her way. And then, as the flames flickered lower, dying out with the first, faint and frosted light, she slipped away, retreating to a secluded bench to catch some brief sleep.

Heather was unaware that her companions had shifted their huddled forms just enough to discretely watch her noiseless departure, or she might have been more careful. A slightly bent, overly padded shadow broke away from the collection of shadows and carefully followed at a distance, watching and waiting until the girl settled herself haphazardly on the far bench. The shade waited, as a predatory bird glides patiently about the clouds, for sleep to come to the unsuspecting teen, and then he made his move.

* * *

She woke to the foul smell of old whiskey, urine and body odour only to see an aged man with peppery, matted hair and beard gently tugging at her pack. He was trying to ease it, inch by inch, from beneath her head without waking her, but he had pulled too hard and her eyes fluttered open.

"What are you doing?!" She clasped the pack to her chest and scampered back against the far corner of the bench.

"Oh come now, Dearie…you don't need that pack. Old Cyrus could use it better than you. Why don't you give it to old Cyrus so he can see what's in it?" The scruffy vagabond reached a sooty and mud-caked claw toward the dangling strap of the nearly empty pack and Heather slapped it away desperately.

"Don't touch me or I'll…"

"You'll what, Dearie?" His drink-fogged eyes narrowed with meanness and he reached for her again.

This time the shift happened quickly and without warning. Heather had no time to prepare as the thing within her launched her body forward with a desperate and vicious insanity. She scratched and bit, slapped and punched, screamed and cursed with a fury that, even through the haze of alcohol, struck fear in the old man. He scrambled backward, landing hard on his rump in the crystallized grass. Crab-walking furiously, the terror drove him, still beating and slapping and kicking until he turned, leapt to his feet with an agility that surprised the audience of tramps and hobos and the few early rising joggers, and bolted to the far end of the park to lick his wounds.

The others stepped back, still watching, wide-eyed with shock, as Heather raged from tree to tree, biting storm-pruned branches, kicking at benches, screeching maniacally. Drool flew from her mouth and splattered her clothes and hair. Her hands were bleeding, but she felt nothing as she cursed and ranted and threw things. And then she calmed. And lay down on her bench. And slept. No one approached the girl with the backpack for the rest of that day.

She remembered nothing but the face of old Cyrus. She knew the fit had come and gone by the evidence of her torn nails and the cuts and bruises that covered her. She knew by the fear in the others' besmudged faces as they kept their distance and threw the occasional furtive glance her way, starting nervously as her gaze wandered in their direction.

She shivered again and decided to get up. Taking her pack, she trudged to the public washroom and began her morning ritual of cleaning, tidying, and spot washing her clothes. Each morning, she washed the previous day's clothes in the sink and then stood patiently drying them under the hand blower. She was in the process of carefully folding her jeans when someone shuffled in behind her.

"You look pretty rough this morning. Not sleep well?"

Heather looked around in surprise. A small woman in her forties leaned against the doorframe and watched her cautiously. She smiled an encouraging grin and shrugged as she turned to look at her dishevelled reflection in the cracked mirror.

"It's not the Hilton. That's for sure."

"No, it ain't that." The woman's voice rasped from smoking the remains of too many castaway cigarette butts. Her hair was hacked short but bore the look of little washing. It would have been a nice nut brown in another life but was too grungy to be anything other than mousy. Her face was drawn thin but didn't show signs of drug use. It was a pretty face, in spite of her underfed appearance, with ocean-grey eyes that were large and round. She was bundled well in old ratty men's clothing stuffed with newspaper, and she held a neatly folded moth-eaten blanket, in front of her.

"That was quite a show you put on this morning. We've never seen old Cyrus so scared before. What was that?"

Heather's shoulders slumped and she dropped her gaze to the stained and cracked tile floor.

"I don't know what to call it other than a fit. That's what my parents called it. They just happen sometimes. I can't control them. If I could, I wouldn't be here." This last was said resentfully. Heather met the woman's glance in the mirror with a challenge and a lift of her stubborn chin, and the woman chuckled.

"You're a feisty one, that's for sure. Me and the gang..." she gestured with a jerk of her head, "figured it was something like that. We thought we'd welcome you to the group and we thought you might need a blanket. We bin watching you since you came to the park and we're all pretty surprised you've made it this far on your own. You looked a little too pampered at first but we're all pretty impressed." She thrust the filthy rag forward, eyebrows raised in hope that Heather would welcome the friendly gesture.

Heather sighed and took the gift, gratefully smiling in return. She had never had someone try to befriend her after one of her fits. Usually people deserted her when her volatile side reared its ugly head. The woman waited patiently for her to finish her morning grooming before turning and slipping from the rank washroom. Heather briskly packed up her meager belongings and tagged after her new friend, a glimmer of hope putting a small spring into her step.

Not everyone in the ragtag group was interested in getting to know Heather. There were some who stayed to the fringes of the group, avoiding her gaze, still uncertain and afraid. Others flat out ignored her, content to be in their own little worlds, but for the most part, she was welcomed openly. The old man who had started it all sat glumly at the far end of his own bench muttering angrily under his breath. Each new phrase was punctuated with a furtive glare in her direction, but he dared not speak openly for fear of unleashing the little demon again.

Heather recognized him immediately and her face reddened with embarrassment. Small glimpses of her attack flitted briefly through her mind, scandalizing her with their violence, and she hesitantly made a beeline to his lonely perch. He shifted uneasily when the young girl approached cautiously, throwing a wary look over his shoulder at her.

Heather had been taught manners. She had been taught to forgive. She had been taught mercy for those with less, and although it hadn't sunk in that she had no more than he, she remembered those lessons driven into her by caring parents. She stood for a few minutes, staring uncertainly at the crisp grass, shifting from one chilled foot to the other.

"What do you want?" the old man grumped at her, "Are you here then to scare me off again? Did you want old Cyrus to look like an even bigger fool?" He turned a hunched shoulder to her.

"No sir, I came to apologize. I can't help it. The fits come and go whenever they want and I can't do anything about it. But you shouldn't have tried to steal my pack. It's all I've got."

Silence settled for a few brief moments and then Cyrus turned to stare at her with unveiled scepticism. Apologize? That was the last thing the dirty old tramp had expected. His eyes narrowed as he scouted her from head to toe. She was still relatively clean and very pretty. He smiled a gap-toothed smile, suddenly, and shuttled his old and weary frame around as an idea wedged into his addicted brain.

"Fits, you say? Maybe old Cyrus could help you with that. But you're right about the pack. Old Cyrus shouldn't have tried to take it. I just wanted to see inside, though. But I shouldn't have scared you like that, young as you are. Are we friends now?"

Heather nodded and thrust her hand forward in an offer of friendship. She recognized, as young as she was, that she'd need all the friends she could get, no matter how unusual. The old man shook the outstretched hand tentatively, still afraid of the young girl, but he knew someone who might be interested in her beauty…in exchange for a reward. Cyrus smiled to himself as he watched the girl settle herself among the collection of misfits of which he was a part.

No one noticed when the old man disappeared. He seldom participated in the conversations even when he did hang around. He was a drifter, coming and going as he pleased, sometimes staying for a few weeks and then leaving again. The motley group of people settled on the grass around the bench and spread out their modest scraps to eat, each watching the others with a caution born of having to defend every mouthful they found.

The rough-looking woman who had offered the blanket settled somewhat protectively beside Heather and handed her a crust of stale bread. Heather was famished and gratefully accepted the scrap, stuffing it into her mouth eagerly.

"So, what's your name? I'm Hildy. That's Shorty and her dog, Whip. Jimmy's the one missing the eye. Lost it in a gambling debt. He wouldn't pay so the guy said an eye would cover the costs. Sure gave up gambling after that, he did. He looks mean but he's harmless. Give you the shirt off his back if he thought you needed it. I think he kind of likes me." She nodded to the bald, skinny man with the puckered eye socket. A dirty red bandanna covered his head and his teeth hadn't seen a toothbrush for quite some time. He smiled shyly at Heather as he held the small mongrel while the dumpy old woman settled her creaking bones on the bench beside him.

Heather warily eyed the next member of the group. He was not much older than she but had shifting, restless eyes the colour of water, bloodshot and vacant. His hair would likely be white if it weren't for the grease and dirt. His skin had a sickly, sallow cast to it and he sniffed his runny nose regularly, indicating that the lad had a liking for cocaine. Hildy followed Heather's stare and snorted.

"That's Chuck. He's trouble so steer clear. And don't go getting messed up in the crap that he's using. It'll kill you…or it'll let one of them fits loose like never before maybe." She said this in a loud whisper meant only for Heather's ears but it was loud enough for all to hear. Chuck was oblivious to it as he settled in to enjoy his most recent snort.

"I'm Heather. Why are you all here? You don't seem…you know…" she didn't know what to say but Hildy finished it.

"Retarded? Stupid? No, most of us aren't missing much upstairs but we've all had things happen that made living difficult in the world you know. It's safer to live this way than to live with what we left. Shorty there…" she nodded at the old woman who sat rocking her dog and singing a lullaby "…we don't even know her real name. She just showed up one day all starry-eyed and lost looking. For years she never said a word and then one day Whip showed up, half-starved, and she started talking to him as though he was a person. Ain't that right, Shorty? Why don't you tell Whip what happened? He forgets." Hildy winked aside to Heather and settled back to watch.

The rocking and singing stopped and Shorty looked down at the dirty canine. Grey tangled curls surrounded a plump and fragile face. Her eyes shone with a mild craziness that every so often gave way to lucid moments. Folds of wrinkled, grimy skin flapped about her neck above the collar of an ugly purple ski jacket that she had found in a garbage can. She wore what looked like a wool skirt but was in fact an old blanket that she had altered to fit her plump waist. Her feet were hidden in the great depths of oversized rubber boots stuffed with rags to keep them on.

"You remember, don't you, Whip? She drowned and I was there. My little grandbaby drowned and they said it was my fault 'cause I answered the phone. But we know, don't we? It wasn't my fault. She wandered off to see the butterfly…and drowned. It wasn't my fault, was it Whip, dear? You know…" the feeble voice faded off into silence and Heather wiped away a tear. She realized she belonged in this group of broken and frail misfits and turned to hear Jimmy's story with a new understanding of what brought people to hide within the back alleys and foul corners of large cities.

"I had a job in a big office building. Stress and lots of money—too much money. I couldn't stay. I couldn't breath anymore. I couldn't stand the pressure. My boss was yelling and I just walked out the door and kept walking. I saw Hildy here in the park, what, eight years ago?—and she looked so happy and free. I won't leave here alive if I can help it." Heather was shocked at how determined he sounded. She had expected them all to be sad, but Jimmy seemed to be right where he wanted to be.

Hildy cleared her throat and looked at Chuck with pity. He sat staring off into space, eyes glazed over and nose running freely.

"That one had a poppa no one would want. He asked him to do things for him—to him—which no poppa should ever ask from their child. The boy didn't even know it was wrong until he got caught trying it on a girl at school. They threw him into a group home and he ran away. He snorts that garbage so he can forget. Old Cyrus…well, he won't tell none of us what put him on the streets. We figure it was just the booze…ain't that right, Cyrus?"

It was then that the group realized the old man had left unnoticed and Hildy's eyes narrowed thoughtfully. Heather scanned the group again, seeing them all in a different light. They were people who hurt inside, like her, and for once, she felt a kinship with someone. She had found a place of belonging among the scattered people of society.

"What about you, Hildy?" she was almost afraid to ask as she watched the worn face carefully. Hildy kept her voice neutral and lifted dead eyes skyward.

"I was born on the streets. My mother was a hooker. She didn't love me 'cause I was a nuisance. She tried to sell me so she could get money. She beat me when I didn't give the men what they wanted. I was younger than you when I ran. I know how to survive and I wouldn't go back to that life if you tried to force me." She turned her weary eyes back to Heather. "You stick by me, kid, and I'll look after you…and watch out for that Cyrus. He comes and goes and would sell his mother for a drink."

Heather nodded, grateful that she had found a friend like Hildy.

Four

THE SUN WAS UP, NO LONGER ANGRY and red, warming the cool landscape. The ice had disappeared from the lake's edge and the deep slate-coloured water lost the fairyland quality of earlier. A moist breeze swooped in off the lake and kicked up the leaves that had already migrated from the tree branches above, swirling them in graceful pirouettes around Heather's head. The rain would come soon, its icy cold pelting the lake and stripping more foliage from the already partially denuded trees.

It was the same season. The season of death. Death of the trees and flowers, death of summer, death of childhood, death of hope. She shook her head and settled on a bluish rock under a half-naked birch tree. No, that wasn't true. Hope wasn't dead. It could lay dormant for years, but it could never truly die.

Heather thought her hope had died that winter so many years back. She would have traded so much to be with her family, but that was not to be. But she had Hildy. She smiled with a gentle fondness at the remembrances of her unusual friend.

She had learned street wisdom and survival from Hildy—and she had learned the true meaning of loyalty. In hindsight, the older woman was a miraculous gift from the divine God who loved her. She saw that clearly now, but back then, Heather couldn't see God's hand in much. She hadn't learned about His grace and love and saving power—yet.

Chapter Four...

Slavery

HEATHER'S LIFE SETTLED INTO a regular routine. She had digressed from job-hunting to merely surviving the harsh winter in the big city. Food became scarce as people moved their eating out of the park and into homes and restaurants. That meant the group needed to scatter and pick through the dumpsters that huddled behind the eateries and supermarkets. The tougher ones got the better garbage, leaving the greasy spoons and fast food joints to the weaker and more timid. The working class, for the most part, chose to ignore the suffering of the lost. That meant that little pocket change made its way into the hands of the cold and hungry cast-offs.

Shorty had found an old shopping cart with one side missing. She improvised with a cardboard box wrapped in plastic and was designated "the driver." So thrilled was she with her find that she talked unceasingly to the doting mutt who sat, like royalty, in the front of the cart, tongue lolling as he watched her attentively.

Hildy and Jimmy did most of the dumpster digging, handing any precious cargo to Heather, who would place it in the cart to take back to whatever shelter or park they would stay at for the night.

For the most part, Chuck would shift back and forth between the world of drug dependency—the haze brought on by the substance of choice—and the desperate reality where he struggled to find another high. On the days he was stoned, the boy would sit in the park and stare into the distance, oblivious to the ministering hands of Hildy, Jimmy, and Heather. On his way down from a high, he would shuffle along behind his companions, eating what he could, hoping to find something to sell for his next fix.

On occasion the small group would be challenged for the cart's contents and Hildy and Jimmy would show their true cunning, honed by past experience on the brutal and unforgiving streets. Jimmy would ease his way to the cart, taking a firm grip, and slowly turn it to angle toward the closest exit while Shorty scooped up her dog, muttering angrily to herself as she waddled quickly away from the coming confrontation. She would casually take Chuck by the arm, pulling the sluggish boy with her, knowing they might need to make a speedy escape.

Heather would join Jimmy at the cart and drop her hand into her jacket pocket, easing the Swiss army knife open with one hand. Her combat skills were nonexistent, but she was more than willing to protect what was theirs. Hildy was the most surprising of all, for tucked neatly into the side of her calf-length boot was a knife sheath that cradled a sharp and dangerous six-inch blade. Where she got it from, no one knew. It seldom saw the light of day, but when it did, the woman became an object of fear to those on the receiving end of its quick and deadly point.

Just the sight of it convinced most to back away, unwilling to lose a piece of hide, but once, Heather witnessed the sorry battle between her friend and an overly persistent bully who was certain his size tipped the balance. She shuddered as she watched fearfully, while Hildy, eyes flat and focused, darted and flitted about the raging bull of a man, carving and hacking ruthlessly until he finally gave up, having bled enough for one day, and quickly backed out of the alley.

Jimmy often stood, poised and ready, fighting only when Hildy thought she really needed help. He had learned years earlier that, with knife, she could dispense street justice far quicker than he could with fist. It had been a nonverbal agreement from the very beginning that he wouldn't interfere unless she wanted him to. And then Jimmy would jump in, fist swinging, with equal ferocity. They hadn't yet had to give up the choicer dumpsters.

Once a pimp approached Heather, something Hildy had warned the girl to expect. The girl had a fresh and innocent beauty that men would pay well for, and Hildy seldom let her out of her sight, knowing that she could be taken quickly.

But winter had a way of pushing a person to their absolute limit. In the colder months people wasted less, making the pickings scarce. The gang had decided to spread out, each taking a different alley, to pick through the garbage for their badly needed food. Hildy, ever alert to possible dangers, sent Heather into a blind alley, taking its mate on the opposite side of the road. She warned the girl to scream loudly if she met any trouble, but Heather assured her it was an unnecessary warning.

The older woman didn't notice the young man, clothed in colourful suit and hat, slip into the alley with his large and muscular friend. But then she heard a familiar screech and hit the pavement running, knife at the ready.

The scene that met her relieved her only a little as she recognized the animal cunning on her young friend's face and a snarl on curled and cursing lips. Heather's fit was in full swing and the fancy-dressed pimp held his arm gingerly while his companion tried to work his way to her side. Hildy realized, by the strange angle, that the man's arm was badly broken and she shuddered at the force it must have taken to do it.

Prepared to assist, the older woman was completely taken aback when Heather, eyes gleaming maniacally, launched herself at the bigger man, hitting, kicking and biting with a fury that surpassed that of a cornered badger. She had found an old spade and was swinging it, with force and accuracy, at the man's head. It was all he could do to cover himself with a protective arm, backing away from the wicked onslaught in fear.

Both men stood together, unaware that Hildy waited behind them while they took part in a hurried conference, eyes never leaving the hissing and growling creature who beat the brick walls with her weapon. And then they eased back, startled at Hildy's presence but not stopping as they worked their way from the alley, the smaller man holding his arm carefully.

Hildy stepped aside, blade in hand and eyebrow raised warily as they passed her, shaking their heads in disgust.

"Could never use that one. She'd kill her customers and then turn on me when I wanted my money. Forget her. We'll look somewhere else." Word spread fast that Heather was not someone to be fooled with. People steered clear.

As the days shortened, drawing the arctic cold closer to their territory, Heather mastered the art of insulating with paper. She was learning quickly, watching her friends in their forays through the back alleys and parking lots of the sprawling city. Anything that could be stuffed into clothing was snatched up eagerly and manners soon disappeared in the struggle to keep warm.

They knew all the soup kitchens, manned by kind and generous folk, and moved from line to line while the winter progressed around them. Savouring the warm and tasty broths and the accompanying chunks of bread, they lived from day to day, grateful for each morsel of food. Their feet were soggy most of the time as the deep snow wedged into cracked shoes and worn socks. The skin around her toes was swollen and cracked and Hildy constantly fussed over her, trying to keep her feet from festering. People came and went from the larger group of vagrants but the five stuck close together.

December dropped upon them with all its glitz and glamour and they enjoyed a delicious turkey dinner at "Christ's Mercy," a nondenominational homeless shelter in the heart of the city's poorest district. Christ's Mercy was a haven of contradiction, really. It was one of the few places in the city where pimps, vagrants, hookers, and gang members could all come together with doctors, lawyers, housewives, and business people to interact without violence or judgment. Only a small handful of workers were paid employees. The rest volunteered, enjoying the task of getting to know society's unwanted while feeding and caring for them. A few members of the police force were known to participate, making some of the less savoury characters a bit nervous on occasion.

Heather didn't know places like this existed until her friends had dragged her into one. Her anxiety over being recognized was unfounded, so complete was her transformation to vagabond. She had long given up keeping clean. Wet hair and skin was cold hair and skin. Her dirt-smudged face was no longer recognizable. She had even been befriended by a husky young police officer who offered her a bowl of warm oatmeal as she waited patiently in the food line. She figured he had no clue as to her age or her identity and since he was quite willing to offer her a friendly hand without judgment or questions, she allowed a tentative friendship to start.

She had seen her own missing child poster once and her heart lurched at what she had left behind. It had taken great effort to simply turn her back and walk on, and no one had commented on the tears cutting tracks through the grime on her cheeks. That afternoon, she escaped to a dead end alley and had a fit, rousing the suspicion of one or two tomcats and a smattering of rats, but no people. No one questioned her when she returned to the park hours later, scratched and bitten. Hildy had wrapped her in a blanket and held her, rocking gently while the girl wept bitterly.

March was a bleak month, with temperatures dropping down to minus eighteen, driving the homeless into the shelters, airports, and bus stations in droves. Some spent the nights sitting on sewer vents along the back streets, soaking up the warm, reeking steam, tolerating the stench of sewage. Others died, their faces frozen into the horror of total abandonment.

Usually death was a blessing, taking with it the addicted who found life too hard to bear, hiding in the substance of choice, wanting and begging for it all to end.

It was a lonely, cruel way to end a life, poor and shattered as it had been, for though the pain ceased, it also destroyed the faint light of hope that flickered patiently within the depths of each human soul.

It was at Christ's Mercy where Heather bumped into old Cyrus again. He carried with him the ever-present stench that accompanied a drunk, and he was shaking with a combination of alcohol withdrawal and the cold. His dirty and matted mustache covered his upper lip, but the lower protruded enough to show the tinge of blue that marked the need for immediate warmth, and he huddled at the edge of the room, talking in undertones to a lean, well-groomed young man.

*   *   *

Hildy hadn't seen the hobo talking to the slick-looking young man in the back corner of the warm dining hall or she would have never left Heather's side. Instead, she got up and pushed her way through the crowd to use the restroom at the opposite end of the room. Shorty and Jimmy waited patiently in line for their portion of food, leaving Heather alone at the table. Cyrus jumped at the opportunity to speak to the girl without the hovering presence of the other three. He was no fool. He had seen how they protected her, most of the time without her even being aware of it. With caution, he eased through the crowd to her empty table.

"It's been a long time, Dearie. How are ya doing?" His voice was smooth and friendly and Heather's face lit up in a smile of recognition.

"Hey, Cyrus, how are you?" She patted the chair next to her, not noticing his furtive glance toward the restroom and food line before he settled himself.

"I'm good, but I can't talk long. Do you still have them fits?" Heather nodded warily, suddenly unsure of the conversation's direction.

"I have a friend who says he can cure you from them. He's a special kind of doctor. Heard about you and wants to meet with you. He's sure he can fix you up proper. Are you interested?"

Heather blinked vacantly, certain she hadn't heard him correctly. Was there a cure? Could she trust anyone who was a friend of Cyrus? A battle began in her mind, pulling her back and forth, screaming for her to leap at the chance/whispering caution.

Cyrus shifted his weight impatiently.

"I ain't got all day. Are you coming?"

He didn't wait for an answer but rose and headed for the hall's exit. Heather was young—and naïve. She glanced at the vacant hall that led to the restrooms, hoping Hildy would appear so she could offer guidance. Then her gaze drifted to Jimmy and Shorty and then back to Cyrus' retreating form. Making her choice quickly, she grabbed at the small hope the old man offered, and rose, following the rank odour that wafted behind him as he squirmed his way through the assortment of people.

Heather knew in a vague way that the young smooth-talking man wasn't to be trusted, but it was too late once she had settled herself in his fancy car "to talk." At first, she had panicked when his driver started the engine and pulled away from the curb, but his gentle voice and calming manner, combined with the car's heating system, soon helped her to relax.

She gaped openly when they pulled up in front of an apartment building in one of the better parts of town and he opened the door for her to step out.

"I just thought we could go up to my apartment for a few minutes. I've forgotten a few things and I thought you might like to clean up a bit before we started your treatment."

Heather nodded slowly, caution still prodding her from its home in the recesses of her brain. The apartment was spectacular in its opulence and she was quite easily convinced to hop into a warm bubble bath for a while. She carefully locked the bathroom door and began to run the water, closing her eyes and inhaling the steamy warmth. A muffled voice drifted in from the other room.

"There's a robe on the door if you want to hand me your clothes. I'll throw them in the wash while we talk about your treatment."

Heather slipped out of the soiled rags and slipped into the clean, thick robe, pulling it tightly around her. Carefully, she unlocked the door and slipped it open wide enough to toss the bundle out and then she shut the door and locked it again quickly.

She probably took longer than she should have, but it had been ages since she'd last bathed and she just couldn't bring herself to leave the luxuriousness of it. Her hair was clean and shiny again and her face scrubbed rosy. The skin on her hands and feet was wrinkled, but it felt so good after such a long drought.

At last, she pulled herself from the tub's depths, drained the murky water away, towelled herself thoroughly and stepped back into the robe, tying the strap in a firm knot. Cautiously, she cracked open the door and scanned the hallway. From the living room, she could hear calming music playing and she headed that way. The man was sitting in a leather lounge chair, head tipped back and eyes closed, nursing a drink of some sort in his left hand. On the coffee table sat an open can of soda and a plate of cookies. His eyes opened to narrow unreadable slits as Heather entered the room and sat on the edge of the sofa.

"Help yourself." He nodded toward the food and drink set before her and watched with satisfaction as she began to wolf it down.

"I'm Andy. Cyrus tells me you have fits of some kind. He says you get quite violent. Is that right?"

She smiled sadly and nodded as she drained the can. And then the room shifted slightly. That was odd, she thought, and opened her mouth to ask Andy about it. No sound came out and the room shifted again. Andy's face stretched, the smile becoming a wicked grin, and Heather tried to lurch to her feet, aware that something was wrong.

* * *

When she woke again, the room was dark. She had a pounding headache and attempted to roll over. A metallic rattle and the pull on her wrists and feet told her all she needed to know as her aching eyes adjusted to the dark—she was chained to the bed. Fear, like she hadn't known before, gripped her, twisting her stomach into knots, and she realized she was naked. What had happened? She pulled at the handcuffs in a futile attempt to either cover herself or break free, and it was the rattling that brought Andy to the door.

He flipped on the light and leered at her, taking his time to eye her from head to toe. She was outraged, anger churning beneath her fear.

"What are you doing? Cyrus said you were a doctor. Let me go!"

He moved closer in a slow, sensual swagger, reaching out to stroke her shin as he spoke, admiring the near-perfection of her vulnerable form.

"Cyrus was right. I am a doctor…sort of. I have very sick patients who come to me regularly and they want me to make them feel better. I give them whatever they need—girls, booze, cards, a bit of grass—and they pay me well to make them feel good.

"But who makes the doctor feel better when he's not happy?" His leering gaze fixed on her horrified face.

"When Cyrus told me about you, Heather, I knew you were my medicine. Just the thought of the passion and power in one of your…fits…excites me. And I haven't felt excitement in a very long time." His words blended together in a quiet monotony of tone—dead sounding—but each one pierced through her brain, sending a new shock of terror with every syllable, prodding the thing within her to awaken from its heavy slumber and lash out at him.

"I want to see a fit, Heather. How does one happen? Cyrus said you were scared when you attacked him. Do you think I could bring one on?" He moved closer, cupping her face in a soft and well-manicured hand. She began to shake with dread, and for once in her life, Heather begged for the fit to take hold quickly.

* * *

It was morning when she awoke again. She was no longer chained and the robe was tossed carelessly beside the bed. Her wrists and ankles were cut and raw from the chafing of the handcuffs as her fit had tossed and thrashed her within the limits of those confines. Her body was covered with bruises, but she couldn't imagine why. She remembered nothing, but knew what had happened just the same.

She snatched the robe and covered herself, tying the knot firmly again, and then leaned over the side of the bed and threw up.

"That wasn't a very nice thing to do, Heather. Now clean it up."

She looked at the switchblade, resting comfortably in Andy's hand, as he leaned against the doorjamb and cleaned his already pristine fingernails. She devoured a deep, shaky breath to calm herself and huddled at the far edge of the rumpled bed. He tossed a towel at her and she mopped up the small mess, glancing often at the blade as it glittered in his hand.

"Now get back on the bed. We're going to try this again without the cuffs. It might be fun."

Heather's screech surprised Andy as the thing in her dove for the knife. The creature within never felt pain and knew no caution as it flailed and struck and ranted. Andy was quick like a panther and the adrenaline pumping through his body gave him plenty of strength, but he wasn't ready for the insanity that poured itself out at him through this young girl.

They wrestled for several minutes, the knife slashing at the air, flicking back and forth, before Andy shoved her away. He wiped at the blood drawn by claw marks and swore as he dove through the doorway, slamming and locking it behind him. He jumped as she hurled herself at the door with a loud thud and then backed away in fear at the crashing of furniture and screaming of obscenities. He'd never try that again.

Heather awoke on the floor. Her face hurt with a searing pain and she lay in something sticky and wet. The sun shone through the window, mocking her dark and empty world with its persistent and invasive light, and she raised her head and looked around. Warm liquid trickled down her face, dropping with a quiet plop onto the patch of blood on the carpet. The stain was already turning hard and brown, indicating that she had been there for a long time.

She reached a trembling hand up to her face and gently touched the gaping wound that started at the edge of her eye and ended just below her mouth. The tears flowed freely, the salt in them stinging fiercely as it washed through the open gash. She sat up slowly, allowing herself to adjust to the loss of blood and light-headedness. Remembering the survival book, she brought the flaps of skin together and pushed firmly against them, wincing at the surge of pain that roused her brain from its torpid state.

After some time, Heather weakly stood, listing slightly as her head cleared, and stumbled her way to the open dresser. Grabbing a man's shirt, she scanned the room slowly, recognizing her own handiwork. Clothing was strewn everywhere and she collected enough of the scattered and torn articles to cover herself decently. The bedside lamp lay in a heap by the wall, smashed beyond repair. No glass remained in the frame that, the day before, held a mirror. The mattress was half off the bed. She slowly checked all accessible parts of her body for possible damage and, other than her face, was relieved to find only minor scratches and additional bruises.

Heather tentatively tried the door handle and discovered it still locked. In defeat, she turned, leaned against the gouged and scraped barrier, and slumped to the floor to wait, aware of the similarity of her old life. A timid voice called from the hallway.

"Are you finished yet?" It was Andy.

"Yes." Her voice sounded dead in her own ears, "I'm cut badly. I need stitches—and some way to clean up the blood." She couldn't believe how calm her voice was and she struggled to move away from the door as the lock clicked. She remained huddled on the floor, too weak to stand and no longer caring as Andy cautiously approached and stroked her silky red hair.

"Man, baby, you sure are a wild thing, but I do love it!" Heather swung her lethargic gaze toward the man as he stared down at her in awe. "I've never seen such power. It's a real turn on." He shifted his caress from the top of her head to her good cheek and she flinched. Dropping his hand, he stepped back into the hallway, motioning her toward the bathroom.

"Let's get you cleaned up. I'll worry about the carpet later. Obviously you can't go to the hospital cause you're underage and they'll ship you back to wherever you came from. I don't really want to go to jail, either, so why don't we just forget anything happened and start over. I'll fix your face the best I can and you will live with me. No one else wants you. What do you think?"

Had it come to this? Heather hung her head in shame. Here she was, almost fifteen and the only person who wanted her was some high-rolling pimp.

She padded unsteadily toward the bathroom, aware of the young man hovering behind her. She knew she really had no choice. He could easily drug her again and do what he wanted. She shuddered at the memory of lying on the bed in handcuffs, but what other life was there? She was tired of being cold and dirty and alone.

Heather sat on the toilet seat with a thud. She was bone tired and found it easiest to lean her head back against the wall, closing her eyes wearily. The first touch made her wince and then the whole wound went numb.

"What was that?" she opened her eyes to watch as he gently cleansed the gash.

"It's just a little something that one of my girls stole from a doctor's office. He pays her to visit him once a month and she thought it might come in handy. It's freezing. I guess it works, huh?"

Using tape and gauze, Andy closed the gap the best he could and put everything away, neatly, into the medicine cabinet. Helping Heather to her feet, he led her to the living room and eased her onto the sofa. The man confused her enormously. How could someone so violent one minute be so gentle the next? Just like her. Again she hung her head.

"We have to come to some sort of agreement, ok?" Andy sounded so much like a businessman that Heather wanted to laugh—except it wasn't funny.

"What do you suggest?"

"You live with me, and I'll only use you during a fit. Can you tell before it hits?"

This was unbelievable, she thought to herself as she nodded.

"Ok then, it's settled. I'll buy you new clothes and stuff and you've got a good place to stay. I like your fits. What more can you ask for?"

Heather looked away, tears forming in her eyes, but she nodded anyway.

"Good." It was done and Andy rose in satisfaction. "Right now, I gotta check on my girls and make sure they are doing their jobs."

"What do your girls do, Andy?" She was afraid to ask but did anyway.

"I got a nice topless club on the other side of town. It has a little side business that keeps my clients happy…real happy, if you know what I mean. I want you to come with me. We'll get some clothes for you on the way."

Again Heather nodded, and a part of her heart died that day.

Five

THE BREEZE HAD PICKED UP, bringing an arctic chill with it. Heather drew the thick dark wool coat tighter around her, more to guard against the cold memories than the weather. The sun, teasing nature coyly, temporarily ducked behind a stray cloud as it skidded across the otherwise clear sky, and she shivered.

Breathing deeply, she forced herself to relax and began to hum a gentle tune, closing her eyes to revel in the words that floated through her mind on the echoes of the haunting melody of the old Scottish hymn.

"Oh great and mighty God, we come,
To offer up our praise,
For you have seen us in our sin and
Loved us all our days.

Come let us now adore you
With songs of grateful love
For you have sent to all mankind
Redemption from above...
Redemption from above."

Heather let the soothing words waft over the scars in her soul, feeling the love, that she at one time thought had died, burst forth from within her chest. As if in answer to the shiver of happiness in her spirit, the sun glided boldly from behind the lone cloud, bathing her upturned face in its tender and caressing warmth. The tears that suddenly sprung to her closed eyes were joyful as she soaked in the peace and comfort that flooded over her. How could anyone say God was dead?

How had she?

Chapter Five...

Survival

SO MUCH WAS LOST TO HER THE DAY she met Andy. Her innocence was destroyed. Her faith in the goodness of mankind and the hope that she could one day go home withered and died within her, leaving her bitter and cynical of all that appeared good. The final touches of civilization slipped away as Heather settled into the life that was offered her.

Most of Andy's time was spent managing his small empire. He had so much to tend to. He paid for protection, ran the club, monitored the girls, ran a marijuana operation on the side (he didn't like the heavy stuff because it killed off the customers) and avoided the law as best he could.

Heather closed her mind to what happened when her fits took hold. If she knew they were coming, she told him. If she didn't, Andy had his hands full. She remembered none of it and the lack of remembering allowed her to keep her sanity. She enjoyed the new clothes and baubles and the security and warmth in a distant, tainted kind of way. And she felt loved—sort of.

Sometimes she and Andy would walk the streets of the nicer neighbourhoods just as though they were a middle class couple spending a few hours of quality time together. During those times she chose to believe there was some good in him. He fussed over her endlessly in the rare moments they shared in their world of fantasy, buying her whatever met her fancy, cooing over her as though she were a precious treasure. Just when she began to feel she had some worth, a fit would take hold, cruelly reminding her of what it was that Andy valued most in her—the creature that held the power to dominate a human's will.

She occasionally saw the old gang from a distance. Andy didn't want her hanging around that kind of street trash and told her so loudly and emphatically. He obviously forgot she had been of the same species not so long ago. She missed Hildy. The older woman loved her, Heather knew that, and it was that love that the girl sought to protect. She would have disobeyed and visited her if it hadn't been for Andy's threat to "slit the hag's throat," and so instead she chose to avoid her, hoping her friend would forgive her for the abandonment. With each passing day, Heather's heart grew heavier.

On one occasion, she slipped money into an envelope and left it within Hildy's sight, making eye contact first and then dropping it "by accident." No one could blame her for that, could they? Andy never caught on and Hildy nodded briefly in understanding. Heather knew it would be shared between her three old friends and it made her happy to know she was there for someone in this crazy and perverted world.

For the first time since Andy had taken her, she felt purpose. A glimmer of hope flickered briefly in the confines of her chest as she discretely watched Hildy sidle up to the envelope and pocket it, meandering back to one-eyed Jimmy and Shorty, who, upon opening it, gaped at her in shock. Forcing her attention back to Andy, she vowed to leave money for them as often as possible.

For three years, Heather followed the bizarre path of street life, watching from the sidelines as though a spectator at some great sporting event, marvelling at the depravity and ingenuity of mankind in his struggle to survive in a part of the world where the rules weren't clearly defined.

For three years she endured Andy's perversions and affection. Three years. She was seventeen, looked twenty-three and felt ninety. Her fits increased until Andy locked her in a separate room anytime he went out. He was tired of coming home to a destroyed apartment. No longer did he come home to clothes strewn asunder and small knickknacks shattered. She had digressed to using one piece of furniture to mash another. Kitchen utensils became carpenter tools, gouging and chewing holes in walls and counters.

Oddly enough, he never seemed to grow tired of her. The more ferocious her fits were, the more he hovered around her afterward, as though he was afraid to lose her. He could almost smell the presence of the other being as it worked hard to consume her, and he knew that he needed her as much as he needed that evil creature that fought for supremacy within. He loved her, if you could call it love, with a possessiveness that surprised her. He bought her gifts and tended her wounds, talking words of affection as best he could.

Heather probably would have spent the rest of her life there if it hadn't been for a careless moment on Andy's part. The bedroom lock hadn't latched and he was gone for another one of those meetings that she never asked about. She rose and dressed quickly, tired of the four walls that barred her from the freedom she had once known, and slipped out into the hallway. Grabbing a spring jacket, she ducked out of the apartment and dashed to the elevator. She would have walked straight out onto the street, but a thought bounced around in her bored mind and she veered off toward the building supervisor's office. Knocking softly, she ducked her head around the open doorframe and smiled at the old man sitting at his desk, eyes glued to the sports channel on his portable TV.

"Hi, Sam. Do you know where Andy went? He left this morning and I thought I'd go for a walk."

The older gentleman, well acquainted with the strange couple on the top floor, lifted a bushy grey eyebrow and nodded.

"Yep, he said he was goin' to the club. Had some business to tend to. Do you want me to call a cab?"

Heather shook her head, politely declining the offer. She'd had enough of confining spaces and wanted the fresh air. The old man shrugged, turning his watery eyes back to the battling figures bouncing around on the field before him.

It took a half-hour to reach the club and she could feel new energy coursing through her. Her lungs tingled with the freshness of unfiltered air, and she tossed her hair back and put her face to the sky while she waited for the crosswalk light to change. She would have to talk to Andy about letting her go for walks when he went out. Maybe he'd walk with her again. It had been awhile since their last stroll.

It wasn't difficult getting into the club, as Heather was known as one of Andy's longest lasting pets. The burly, barrel-chested guard scrambled to his feet to open the door for her. She wasn't expected, but maybe Andy had called her. He shrugged and watched her, a poorly hidden leer plastered on the ugly mug, as she strolled into the entranceway.

It was early in the afternoon and the club didn't open until dinnertime, leaving Heather to wander down empty and hollow sounding halls toward the far end of the building, the soft clacking of her heels echoing off the cement block walls. As she neared the collection of rooms sometimes used as office space, she could hear the increased ruckus of men's voices raised in shouts. Turning the last corner, Heather was surprised to see a crowd of Andy's henchmen in a tight circle, looking down at something on the floor, shouting and jeering in the dim lighting of the back stage room.

Her blood ran cold at the first feminine scream as it echoed harshly down the empty halls and she cringed at the sharp slap as a hand made contact with a face. The men laughed and Heather slowed as she recognized Andy's voice, vicious and loud.

"Why, you piece of trash. How dare you slap me! I'll teach you to steal money from me. You think you can get tips and I won't find out about it? Maybe I'll just take my own pay now."

The scream shattered against the concrete walls again, cutting a vicious path through the receptors in Heather's brain and she reacted instinctively. She forcefully pushed her way through the wall of muscle, ignoring the grunts and protests, and gasped at the sight before her. Already, Andy had the woman half stripped and his hand rose and fell rhythmically as he batted her about the face. Blonde hair was wrapped tightly around his clamped fist and blood trickled from her split lip and crushed nose. Bruises and welts were beginning to show themselves across the naked upper torso, marring the perfection of the too-young body.

It wasn't the thing within Heather that exploded all over the unsuspecting tyrant. The dam that had held all the hurt and anger of seventeen years burst upon Andy, knocking him to the floor beside the nearly unconscious stripper.

The men encircling them watched in shock as the little red haired hellcat went berserk all over Andy's back. His arms were clasped behind his neck in an effort to protect his head and his muffled command shook the bystanders into action.

"Get her off of me, will ya?"

And then the fit moved in and they were doubly shocked at the power and strength and vulgarity and violence that propelled her at them. It was all they could do to stay out of her reach, never mind pin her down.

One man drew a gun, so fearful was he of the raging beast before him, but Andy cuffed him on the side of the head, shouting maniacally.

"Don't hurt her, you idiot. She's my woman. You shoot her and I'll kill you!"

She thrashed and struck, oblivious to any answering pain, and the demon within saw the opening created by her well-aimed kick. She bolted past the doubled-over giant and ran, with abandon, legs churning and lungs bursting, down the corridor to the front door.

Once again, the guard was jolted upright as the crazed woman threw herself through the doors and, screeching and swearing, hair dishevelled and sweat pouring down her face and throat into her neckline, ran down the middle of the sidewalk.

Heather moved blindly, dodging people and traffic, unseeing and uncaring. People dove for cover as she continued babbling loudly and crashing against anything in her path. She would have been easy to follow if the crowd hadn't closed in behind her, stopping to gape as the wild woman stumbled her way down the subway stairs.

A part of her mind remembered the labyrinth that ran below the concrete jungle and this part of her sanity directed her down twists and turns until she could no longer hear the men pursuing her.

The fury was receding as Heather surfaced once more into a darker part of the city. She was tired—so tired—but recognized the place. She pushed herself until she found what she remembered and slipped furtively into the dead end alley, hunkering down behind the filthy dumpster to sleep.

She slept for nearly two days and when she woke, she remembered enough, and cried. It seemed her life was full of crying, and this once she gave in to it fully, allowing the tears to cleanse much of her pain. She had seen herself in the hapless circumstances of the dishonest stripper. Andy didn't love her. He didn't know how to love. All he understood was power and satisfaction, and he, like any predator, took pleasure in sucking the life-blood from other living creatures.

But Andy didn't like to lose and he wouldn't be happy that she had left him. It was fine for him to throw someone away like yesterday's garbage, but Heaven help the one who tried to discard him.

Heather took a handful of dirt and rubbed it over her face. The quicker she changed her looks, the safer she would be. Slyly, she pulled herself into the open dumpster and scrounged through the refuse shamelessly until she found a lid from a tin can. Testing the edge, she deemed it satisfactory and began to hack at her long hair until no more than an inch's length covered her head. Digging further, she came across an old men's shirt, previously used as a rag, and donned it overtop her t-shirt. In the same bag of castaways was an old tablecloth, easily transformed into a skirt, and a cap, finishing her ensemble and completely changing her looks.

She spent another week living from that dumpster until she felt it was time to move on. She filled two plastic shopping bags full of junk, hoping to add to her disguise that really wasn't a disguise, and she shuffled down the alley.

Heather took her time trying to reach her destination. She had padded her clothes with rags, making her appear plump, and walked, bent, dragging one foot slightly. She kept her head down, the battered baseball cap jammed on tight. A piece of mud and ash mixed together formed a mole, which she had stuck to her chin. Hopefully, it would keep people from looking at the broader features of her face.

She shuffled aimlessly down the crowded street, stopping from time to time to nonchalantly pick through the cans of rubbish placed beside occasional light posts. Rush hour was Heather's favourite time of day because it allowed her to hide in plain sight. Weaving down alleys and back streets, she drew upon the skills Hildy had taught her and the things she had learned while living with Andy.

Once, she thought she was done for when Andy's car pulled to the curb in front of her. Two of the men from the club climbed out and leaned against the car, scanning the crowd. She stayed put, mumbling to herself in a raspy voice while she picked through the garbage can nearby.

She almost dropped her packages and gaped when Andy, tired and haggard, appeared in the doorway of the building beside her, passed her without a second look, and climbed onto the car's rear seat. He never spoke. His face was drawn and angry. She almost buried her face in the garbage can when he looked her way, focusing on her momentarily, and then the car pulled away from the curb and was gone.

It took some time for Heather's heart to stop pounding. She stayed put until she could breathe slowly again and then continued at a faster pace toward her destination—a place where she hoped she could be safe once more.

It took her two days of discretely worming her way through the crowded city before Heather safely reached the park. It felt like coming home. She stood a block away and searched the crowds for Andy's people. There. The guard—what was his name?—who always tended the door at the club. He had been the one who had allowed her past and he was probably regretting that decision by now. No doubt Andy had told him to either find Heather or he would be a dead man.

He was sitting at a table outside a café across the road from the park, scanning the people's faces and forms. He didn't look happy. What to do? Heather looked longingly at the park and then down at her clothing. She couldn't go back to Andy. He wouldn't be very gentle with her. But then, he hadn't even recognized her from five feet away. She smiled, breathed in a calming breath, and began her slow uneven trek to her haven.

She had gotten across the road to the park's entrance when he caught up with her, blocking her further progress by planting himself between her and her destination.

"Excuse me, miss, but can I talk to you."

Heather didn't dare look up. She wasn't sure when the guard had left the café, but she knew that voice. She continued to stare at the expensive leather shoes in front of her and then a thought occurred to her. She began rocking slowly back and forth, allowing drool to run down the corner of her filthy mouth. With exaggerated slowness she began to talk.

"Who aw wu? I am pwime ministew. I cook at da bank." Her voice was low and raspy and she continued to babble her nonsense, swaying back and forth. She never looked up once, watching the shoes carefully. Reaching out, she began gently patting his suit coat sleeve, knowing that some people are repulsed by the touch of a vagrant. The guard took a step back, pushing her hand away.

Suddenly, Heather let out a startled squeak as two arms gently draped themselves around her shoulders. A familiar voice drifted calmly from beside her as she felt herself being turned.

Her companion looked back over his shoulder, apologizing to the guard as they walked away. She continued to weave back and forth, babbling nonsense under her breath and stared at the grass at her feet as her saviour continued.

"She's a little touched in the head, sir. Thinks she's the Prime Minister or a cook or something. She's been like this for years. I'll keep her away from you. Sorry, sir."

He never gave the guard a chance to answer but kept her moving into the heart of the park.

"Just keep moving Heather. He's still watching. I think you have him fooled, but keep going just in case. We can always make a run for it. There, he's heading back to the café but he keeps looking back, so just keep doing what you're doing. Man, you're good and we've sure missed you. That's quite the get-up. Too bad your hair's gone, but that don't matter to us none. Everyone will just be glad to see you back."

The two ducked behind a big maple tree and Heather turned to give Jimmy a big hug. He folded her in a tight embrace and then they resumed their charade until they were well out of sight. Cutting across the park, they ducked behind the public washrooms and followed one of the bike paths until they reached a clump of scrub brush where Hildy stood, tapping one small foot impatiently as she waited for them to arrive.

Upon seeing the ruffian, the older woman launched herself at her with maternal protectiveness, wrapped her in a bear hug, and clung to her, sobbing.

"We didn't know what happened to you. We thought you were dead. I nearly had a heart attack when I saw you walking down the street with that piece of garbage. It didn't take us long to find out what happened after that. Cyrus didn't feel very good for a while. Seems you've hit a soft spot in somebody's heart 'cause when word got out that he sold you to that slime-ball, Andy, somebody went and beat him up. He only showed up here once after that. We made it real plain that we didn't want no traitors in our park. Haven't seen him for a couple years. Hope he died and rotted in some gutter somewhere, the pig."

All of this was choked out between sobs while one-eyed Jimmy stood by, patting one feminine shoulder and then the other. Occasionally, he stopped to wipe at a stray tear that sneaked past his one good eye, and then he would smile widely and pat shoulders again. Even Shorty broke out of her own world for a small time, clasped Heather in a tight hug, looked deeply into her face with serious eyes and nodded knowingly, before waddling her way back to her perch on a large dirty rock.

The emotional reunion continued for some time as each of the four took turns sharing their impressions and reactions until all had been retold, and then Heather glanced around the small clearing, searching for one more face to complete the family.

"Where's Chuck?"

The smiles faded and Jimmy's sigh said enough.

"We lost him last winter. He got so caught up in that crap he was snorting that he started stealing to get more. We tried to keep him out of it but there are just some ghosts that can't be lived with and he had his. His last time, he stole a necklace at a jewellery store. He got a nice load of stash for it. It was supposed to be enough for a few highs but he did it all at once. He got so stoned that he didn't realize when the storm hit. We didn't know where he'd gone or we would've kept him warm. Didn't find him until the spring thaw. He was tucked up under the railway truss over by the warehouses. I guess he didn't feel any pain. What better way to go."

Heather bowed her head and fought with her grief. Such a lost young life snuffed out too soon, and yet, Jimmy was right in one sense. Chuck no longer felt the pain of his abusive father and a mother who turned a blind eye to it. She lifted her head to gaze at the beauty of the trees and gardens around her, her heart moaning against the contradiction of a God who could create such perfection in nature and such cruelty within the heart of mankind.

Jimmy's face was tight as he stared across the park, seeing nothing. He took it hard when he lost a friend and he felt like a failure for not being able to help Chuck. Absently, he reached over and patted Heather's shoulder once more. He wouldn't let that happen again.

Six

HEATHER HEARD HER NAME ECHO hollowly through the cool morning air as it bounced off the rocky foundation around her known as the Canadian Shield. She turned her head and smiled in the direction from whence it came. Fluidly, the young lady rose from her perch by the water and waved at the figure standing on the rough-hewn wooden porch that clung solidly to the residence she had earlier exited.

"Are you coming in for breakfast?"

She smiled tenderly, her gaze unconsciously appraising her friend as the lady stood, well-groomed and younger looking, arms akimbo, expression questioning. The older woman was still mothering her, in her own way, but Heather would never have a problem with that. Turning, she stole one last look at the peaceful scene before her and began her slow trek back up the hill toward the log building burrowed halfway into the side of the hill above her.

"I'm coming, Hildy. Keep your knickers on."

Again, Heather smiled as Hildy, mouse-coloured hair whipping about her head in the growing wind, tisked at her in mock frustration and flounced back into the building, leaving the door open behind her. The younger woman couldn't imagine what her life would have been like if God hadn't placed such a true and faithful person in her path.

The first spatterings of rain plopped against her wool hat and coat, soaking into the rough and heavy fibre, and she picked up her pace, fighting against the increased gravity of the steep path and the wind that had begun to whistle its way around the trees and shrubs which dotted the edge of the path.

She was only a little winded when she reached the empty porch, but she still stopped to rest against one of the log posts that supported the steps, enjoying the weighty sound of the rain as it swooped down upon the dry and hungry countryside, dousing it in its sudden deluge.

She turned her head slowly, surveying all that was before her, and was overwhelmed with the beauty of God's creation in all its varied moods. She sniffed the air with appreciation, enjoying the fresh and cleansing smell of the rain mingling with the kitchen smells wafting through the open door behind her. The water dappled the surface of the lake, rippling it into an aged and wrinkled face while the loons still bobbed and floated on the roughening surface.

When it rained, she thought of Chuck, and all those like him, who had died without hope. It was as though God cried for them, their souls no longer reachable, lost for eternity from Him. It was a season of mourning for those who had turned their backs on His grace and mercy.

Heather sighed with the boy's loss. It could have been her so easily. But for the grace of God and good friends, she could just as easily have been lost in the gaping maw of street living. There were still moments where she pondered the amazing turn of events.

She had been given so much. And deserved so little. What more could a woman ask for?

Chapter Six…

The Road Back

THEY KNEW HEATHER WAS FAR FROM SAFE. Andy and his sadistic henchmen were out there somewhere, still searching, still hoping to find some trace of the vagrant girl who threw fits of insanity without warning. With summer upon them, more people would be outside. More people would interact with the society of wanderers, making it harder for her to hide when she did succumb to the violence that was slowly taking over her life.

Heather embraced the challenge that came with avoiding her controlling and perverted pursuer. She was happy to be back in the park, living a simple life, knowing that someone would guard her when the fits took hold. Hildy had long ago learned to recognize the approach of a fit before it got out of control and Heather knew one was coming when her friends gathered around her, quickly ushering her to a safe and private hollow or back alley.

She seldom caused much damage in the park. The sturdy trees were more than capable of withstanding her most vicious attacks, but it was unsettling just the same. Sometimes she drew a small crowd of spectators, and it was in those times that it was a miracle that Andy never tracked her down. It was hard to overlook someone who had screaming tantrums, threw garbage cans around, and thrashed about in the shrubbery.

Weeks passed into months and months stretched the years out. They relaxed—some. It was not always easy living a life of constant suspicion and fear while struggling to survive. For four years, Heather watched the crowds cautiously and blended in as best she could. And then one day the news came. It arrived on the lips of the least likely carrier, and Cyrus didn't know if he would even be welcome.

At first sight of the feeble alcoholic, Hildy, Jimmy, and Shorty stepped in front of a sleeping Heather. The fit had taken hold of her and held her far longer than usual, leaving her exhausted and weak. Sleep had come quickly, but that was hours ago and they had been hovering over her anxiously since.

Cyrus stood, battered hat in hand, looking repentant before the three guardians. He shuffled uneasily under their protective glares and finally stuttered out what he wanted to say.

"Look, I came to say sorry to the kid…and to tell you all that Andy's in the clink. Has been for a couple of years now. He cut up one of his girls really bad and she died. He didn't realize it was caught on one of his own security cameras at the club and the cops got a hold of it. I didn't know he was so…mean, or I wouldn't have handed her over. I'm different now. I wanted you guys to know. I stopped drinking. Joined a group and got a job washing dishes. Got religion. I want to help."

Skeptical eyes scanned the old man closely, looking for any hint of deception. Hildy shook her head in anger, slowly drawing the wicked knife from its concealed sheath, and holding it loosely by her side. Cyrus wouldn't pull a fast one on her again or he'd find himself missing some skin. To Hildy, the girl was like a daughter, and nothing would separate them ever again if she had any say.

"You haven't really given us much of a reason to believe you, now, have you, Cyrus?"

The old man hung his head in shame and turned the hat in his hand. He was still wearing worn clothes, but they were clean and, for once, his hair was trimmed and combed.

"No I guess I haven't. But I just wanted you to know that, for now, the kid's safe."

A sleepy voice cut into the conversation, turning the three about.

"I believe him, Hildy. Something's different, isn't it, Cyrus?"

Heather pulled herself wearily from the bench and regarded her former Judas with curiosity.

"You look pretty good, Cyrus. What's happened to you?" She circled him, eyeing him from head to toe. The older man no longer smelled foul like cheap whiskey but had the fresher scent of soap. His clothes bore the look of conscientious attention, and although he still sported the wiry and grizzled beard, it was clean and groomed. His eyes twinkled with lucidity and he stood firmly, no longer swaying from the affects of alcohol abuse. He smiled tentatively at her, and for once, the smile reached his eyes.

"I told you I got religion. There's a new boy down at the mission and he talked about forgiveness and that it was for everyone, even trash like me. It took me some time to believe what he was saying, but it's true. I regret what I done, but I'm free from the guilt. I don't drink no more and don't even really want to. He done healed me, child. You could have that too, Heather."

He eagerly searched her face, pleading with her silently, but Heather shook her head sadly. Hildy snorted derisively in the background, crossing her arms defensively, still unconvinced. With a nudge from Heather, she mumbled angrily and grudgingly sheathed her blade in its discreet hiding place, still watching the old man with the eyes of a hawk. Jimmy and Shorty stood there, waiting, not certain what to believe, assessing the new Cyrus with narrow-eyed confusion.

"I'm glad for you, Cyrus, really I am, but…" she hung her head hopelessly, "I don't think your religion can fix my problem."

She looked so lost and forlorn, as though her abandonment was so total that it reached into the ultimate depths of her soul. As she turned to go back to the bench, Cyrus impulsively reached out, gently placing a hand on her arm to detain her.

"But you need to hear about Jesus. He…"

The screech took everyone by surprise and Cyrus jumped back in shock as Heather threw herself to the ground in terrified agony. She writhed and pulled at her hair, moaning and screaming maniacally, all the while glaring at Cyrus with an unearthly hatred. Arms flailed as claw-shaped hands pounded the ground in front of her. Even Hildy was unprepared for the suddenness of the fit.

What happened next was as surprising to the old man as it was to everyone else present. An authority settled over him, cloaking him in a blanket of calmness as he stepped closer.

"I've read in the Bible about this type of thing. I'm not a very strong Christian man so I'm not sure I can do anything, but

I know who can. For right now, we need to get her to the mission. The only way that's gonna happen is if that thing in her settles down—so here goes."

He pulled himself to his full height of a hunched and gnarled five-foot-three-inches, looked to Heaven, and smiled. And then he spoke.

"Dearest Saviour. It's me, Cyrus. I don't know much about this here thing but I know we need to get Heather to someone who does, so I'm just gonna trust you to help me say and do the right things cause I know you're stronger than the creature inside her."

He looked back to the pathetic girl squirming and wallowing in the grass at his feet, gnawing on her own hands and tongue. He then knelt and placed a hand calmly on her shoulder. She winced, letting out a wail of unearthly anguish and tried to crabwalk away from him. He smiled at the memory of himself doing the very same thing several years past, but held fast to his firm grip on her arm. And then the words came.

"Creature, I know you don't belong there, and if I were a stronger believer, I might just take you on. But I know my place just like you need to know yours. So I'm calling on the strength of the Lord Jesus Christ and telling you now to be quiet and still."

His voice was calm but cut the air like a thunderclap and Heather went limp. Hildy and Shorty gasped in unison and Jimmy's eyes narrowed suspiciously. Gnarled old hands that had once eagerly clasped liquor bottles now gently caressed Heather's soft cheek. Cyrus looked up pleadingly at the three faces hovered around as he struggled to lift the unconscious form from the ground.

"Come on guys, can't you just trust me this once? She needs help and they'll help her at Christ's Mercy. I don't think we've got a lot of time. I'll carry her myself if I have to, but it would make it a lot easier if you were inclined to help."

Again Hildy snorted as the three snapped into action.

"If you think for a minute, you old coot, that I'm going to let her out of my sight, especially with you, you're completely crazy." With that, she grabbed an arm and helped hoist the girl over one-eyed Jimmy's strong, wiry back.

Heather stayed asleep through the entire journey to the mission. All the sly and covert pathways were completely abandoned in favour of the most direct route, and the small crowd arrived quickly, ignoring the curious stares along the way.

The young police officer that had tried so hard to befriend a younger Heather opened the mission door for the group and offered to relieve Jimmy of the limp and heavy burden. As much as Jimmy was reluctant to release her into the officer's care, the middle-aged man was not used to carrying such a load so far, and so he shrugged her still form into the young man's waiting arms.

She was placed gently onto a cot in a small room behind the massive kitchens and they waited anxiously while Cyrus went searching for the new pastor. The three tramps watched with a street-born cautiousness as the kind man knelt to cover the comatose figure with a rough wool blanket.

It took some time before old Cyrus, so completely changed, returned with a tall, heavily muscled young man with dark hair. In spite of his size, they knew he was too young to be a pastor. Hildy narrowed her eyes spitefully at Cyrus, her temperature rising.

"Who you trying to scam? That ain't no minister. Even I can tell that. He ain't no more than twenty years old. If you've brought another dirt bag like Andy, I'll skin you alive, you old…"

"Excuse me…" the giant stepped between the two vagrants with a peaceful gesture, his eyes crinkling with a touch of amusement. "You're right; I'm not the pastor. I'm his son, Charlie. And you are?"

The forty-year-old woman eyed him from head to toe, relaxing a little but keeping herself between them and Heather and the attending officer.

"My name's Hildy. I'm like her mother, kinda. Can you help her? She's had these fits since I've known her. She was fourteen when she came to the park and they're getting worse. If you hurt her, I'll…"

The young man smiled at her protectiveness and the lunacy of her threat. She was lucky to top five feet tall and weighed one hundred pounds—maybe. He was six foot four and two hundred pounds of muscle. But he admired the pluck and loyalty she displayed on behalf of the bundle huddled unconscious, facing the wall on the rickety cot behind her. He raised a questioning brow to the police officer who nodded his acknowledgement and rose, stepping far enough away to make room for Charlie.

"I promise I won't hurt her. My dad's gone to the hospital to visit one of the regulars here and said he'd be back soon. I won't try anything without him here, and you're welcome to stay with her through the whole time. I just want to get a look at her, if it's ok with you."

He earnestly scanned the three faces before him while Cyrus hovered in the background, head bowed, whispering quietly to himself. Had the small gang of hobos known that the old man was praying for deliverance and salvation for the souls in that room, they would have dropped on the spot.

Hildy harrumphed and slowly stepped to the side, allowing the gentle giant access to the prone form. He eased her onto her back, pulled the blanket away from her face—and gasped.

"What is her name?"

The voice was suddenly sharp and the blue eyes lost their twinkle, piercing into Hildy's very soul, gripping at her heart with an anxiety and urgency that commanded her to respond. She took a step back at the sudden change of demeanour and glanced uneasily at Cyrus, who continued to mutter to himself, eyes closed.

"She answers to Heather, but I've never known her Christian name. She never told it. Why?"

The lad sat heavily on the floor by the cot, dropped his head into his meaty hands, and began to sob quietly. The unkempt group waited awkwardly, shuffling from one foot to the other. The young officer dropped to a knee beside the weeping lad and rested his own large hand on Charlie's shoulder, waiting patiently for an answer to everyone's unspoken question. Finally he drew in a deep breath, wiped his face on his shirtsleeve, and lifted red-rimmed eyes.

"I think she's my sister."

* * *

Heather was unconscious through the entire introduction. She missed much, but could still manage to hear the voices like one hearing two poorly tuned radio stations at once. The louder voice was the one she was used to, snarling through her mind all the obscenities invented since the beginning of time. But faded and indistinct, she heard the other voices and one in particular, which she was sure she knew.

Something had changed. She had never had awareness of any kind when the thing had taken her and shoved her aside. She had only ever heard its condemning and savage voice. It had dominated her, owning every aspect of her mind and body as it chose. For the first time, it grovelled angrily within, restrained by some unseen hand, allowing Heather to hear faintly.

What she heard shocked her in a far off way; at least she would have been shocked had she been able to fully feel, but comprehension seeped into her subjugated brain enough to allow her a small understanding of the distant voices. She struggled against the tyrant's chains, trying to free herself enough to allow her to reach out to the one voice she heard most clearly of all.

* * *

"And what do we have here now, my friends?" The voice was jolly and deep, matching in every respect, the man it accompanied. He was a bit shorter than Charlie, but thicker, if possible. His rusty hair was very thin and liberally scattered with grey, but the face was young and happy. Deep in the water blue eyes lay a sorrow from a distant time accompanied by unearthly peace. He looked down at his son's tear-streaked face and then caught sight of the young lady asleep on the cot. The smile froze on his face as his eyes darted back to his son, who merely nodded. And then she writhed and moaned. The thing within her was returning to life. Hildy, Shorty and Jimmy stepped back. Whip growled his high-pitched threat and cowered behind Shorty's skirt.

The pastor's eyes welled with tears as he stepped closer to touch his oldest daughter, but she let out a scream and babbled obscenities. He glanced at his son knowingly and nodded. He turned calmly to the three frightened vagrants and cleared his throat, fighting against his own emotional shock.

"I can't begin to tell you all how much I am overwhelmed at seeing my daughter again. It has been seven long years without her. I wish I could take the time to explain everything now, but Heather needs help as you all can see."

Angus lowered himself beside Heather's thrashing form with unrivalled determination. Seven years had gone into the preparation for this moment, and he was eager to see it through.

He turned back to his son, brusquely commanding him to fetch the other clergy members who worked faithfully in the shelter, but her screeching and howling had already attracted their attention and they filed into the crowded room anxiously, waiting—curious. Angus turned pain-filled and pleading eyes toward his brothers in the faith and they silently moved in, placing hands on the struggling form. Charlie rose to his knees, adding his touch. David, the police officer, kept back, leaning against the wall, lowering his head in anticipation of the battle ahead.

And then the prayers began. And the creature within the human shell jumped and thrashed in terror as the group entered the presence of the Great I AM.

"Mighty Father, Creator of all the Universe," the Scottish brogue dipped and rose in its lilting cadence and an unseen presence, overwhelming with its strength, filled the room. Hildy shivered with a sudden fear.

"We are aware of the greatest battle of all—the battle for souls. It is no coincidence that you have, like the Biblical parable, brought the prodigal child home.

"We are so ignorant in our humanness, but you know all that needs to be known. Father, we lift this young daughter to you and ask you to claim her as your own. We don't presume to have the strength to free her from this evil creature..." the struggle within Heather's body intensified as the men prayed over her, "...but you came to earth, died and rose again, conquering death and all its evil beings. Knowing this, we ask you to free Heather from the chains of possession, in Jesus' triumphant name."

Each man took turns praying over the thrashing form, amazed at the tenacity of the evil spirit and shamed at his own weakness. It was, in the end, Cyrus who brought about the healing needed. He was frightened and wide-eyed, unsure of how he could help, when the idea came to him to open his New International Version Bible, rumpled and worn with four years of use.

It took time—and frantic searching—but eventually he grunted with satisfaction when he found the passage he sought. With a clear and ringing voice, the old man stood and read aloud, silencing all in the room.

"The next day, when they came down from the mountain, a large crowd met him. A man in the crowd called out, 'Teacher, I beg you to look at my son, for he is my only child. A spirit seizes him and he suddenly screams…'"

The creature burst forth in Heather's mind, flailing and thrashing at her, begging for the silencing of the words of power that crashed into every corner of the room. The men continued praying, heads bowed and hands firmly placed upon her. There was no debate over right of authority as Cyrus continued reading scripture in his gravelly but purpose-filled voice.

"'It throws him into convulsions so that he foams at the mouth.'"

Heather was twisting and writhing, struggling to lash out at the men whose prayers were storming the gates of Heaven in their fervency.

"'It scarcely ever leaves him and is destroying him. I begged your disciples to drive it out, but they could not.'"

By this time, froth was trickling from the corners of Heather's mouth and she moaned hoarsely, her muscles strained and tense, convulsions wracking her slender form.

"'O unbelieving and perverse generation,' Jesus replied, 'how long shall I stay with you and put up with you? Bring your son here.'

"Even while the boy was coming, the demon threw him to the ground in a convulsion. But Jesus rebuked the evil spirit…"

A haunting scream tore from Heather's throat as she arched stiffly against unseen constraints and her eyes rolled back into her head as it jerked violently from side to side.

"…healed the boy and gave him back to his father. And they were all amazed at the greatness of God."

Silence shredded the atmosphere as the old man straightened his shoulders and looked to Heaven once again.

"Blessed is the word of the Lord through Jesus Christ our Saviour."

And the girl went limp.

Seven

SHE PAUSED INSIDE THE TILED ENTRANCE—heart filled to overflowing—and scanned the room. It had come to life with the loud chatter of the residents. The rich fragrance of fried bacon, sausage, eggs and toast wafted heavily in the warm air, causing Heather's mouth to water in anticipation. Hildy was a surprisingly good cook. Street life had taught her much, but there was a natural skill there that everyone was more than happy to help nurture. All were seated around the oversized pine board table, reaching for the bounty laid upon it and laughing and talking loudly.

Heather's eyes softened as she gazed fondly at each of the room's occupants. She watched contentedly as Hildy bustled around the common room, loading heaps of food on each plate, stopping to joke or admonish each person. She playfully slapped at a hand as it wandered toward the pickle tray prematurely. There were several people Heather almost didn't recognize—so changed were they, who had come from off of the streets of Toronto—and a handful she knew so well.

Her eyes wandered next to Jimmy, clean and red cheeked, at the foot of the table. He sat quietly, watching Hildy as she flitted about the room. A look of adoration was plastered across the clean-shaven face and Heather chuckled. Hearing the sound, the one-eyed man glanced her way, blushing profusely at being caught admiring the housemother so openly, but he winked at Heather and returned to his perusal of the object of his affection.

Heather simply winked back and silently thanked God for such true and loyal friends. For these were the friends who had stood with her when it was a danger to do so. It was they who had taught her to survive, guarded her with their own lives and helped her begin her journey home.

Chapter Seven...

The Awakening

WHEN ASKED WHAT IT FELT LIKE, Heather would later refer to the casting out of the demon as waking from a very long dream—an evil, terrifying dream, full of torment and self-loathing, malefic and spiteful creatures, and utter loneliness.

One moment she was struggling, as though through quicksand, to free herself from the dark and horrifying clutches of a spirit so strong that she was sure she would be hurled into insanity. The next, she was awake and gasping in sweet, fresh air, the creature cowed and whimpering as a greater, gentler being ushered her soul out of its reach and into the clear beauty of freedom.

She sat up and looked about her, momentarily disoriented. There was Hildy, clutching Jimmy's arm in terror. Jimmy himself stood with his mouth agape, stunned beyond belief. Shorty huddled in the corner with a barking and snarling Whip, rocking back and forth and humming tunelessly, her eyes wild. The clerics that she knew only vaguely knelt around her, hands resting on her shoulders. Over by the wall David still stood, watching her with awe. But it was Cyrus that drew her attention.

The wizened senior stood, face turned Heavenward, eyes closed, wearing such a look of beautiful peace and contentment that it made Heather's very soul cry out in hunger. And then she returned her gaze to the men around her and one, in particular, stood out to her.

"Dad?"

The shock registered in her voice. Where did he come from? What was he doing here? Her gaze whipped around to the young man with the dark hair and tear-streaked face.

"You're..."

"Charlie." The voice was quiet, deep and smooth, and Heather gaped in awe at her little brother.

Angus was too choked up to speak, and when huge tears began streaming a course down Heather's face, he merely sat beside her, pulled her to himself and rocked her soothingly, his own tears dampening her cropped, filthy hair. Her mind jumped back to her early childhood as though she had never left and she snuggled her face into his shirt and wept bitterly.

Discreetly, the leaders of the shelter rose and left, not wanting to interrupt the bittersweet reunion. The gang of tramps hovered off to the side, unsure of what to do. Hildy's chest tightened as she realized the full impact of what was taking place. She was going to lose Heather again. Jealousy and resentment battled fiercely with the love that she had for the girl, and she finally slipped from the room to think it all through, her friends following dazedly.

Later, Hildy would marvel at the kindness and gentleness poured on her by those who had witnessed the miracle—especially Cyrus. Jimmy would have been more attentive, but he had his own thoughts to sift through. It was almost too much for Shorty, who shrank further into her imaginary world.

Angus finally rose to his feet, pulling his daughter and son with him.

"I think we all have stories to share. If you would permit me to, I'd like to go first. Why don't we find some place where we can sit comfortably and uninterrupted while we talk."

Heather and Charlie both nodded dumbly and followed the man who seemed to be able to take everything in stride. He led them past the common room, sparsely populated with the nameless lost souls of the streets, to the offices and small apartments in the back.

Finding an empty room, the three entered, Charlie closing the door to ensure the privacy they all craved. Heather settled into a battered lounge chair, ignoring the musty smell as her gaze swept the dull and worn paneled room. Disbelieving eyes rested on her father's face, older and a bit more worn, but set with a conviction that made her heart beat faster.

"When you left us, Heather, it tore our world apart. For weeks, we searched the streets of London, hoping to catch a glimpse of you, afraid you were dead. We phoned the hospitals and morgues for months, relieved that your name was not listed, terrified that you were hurt and couldn't get help. I nearly went insane those first months. If it weren't for your mother, I don't know where I'd be now.

"I started drinking. I felt like such a failure; I hadn't protected you and I wasn't able to fix it. Your mother was amazing. She never gave up hope that you would be found.

"I got drunk once and I…I…" he looked out the window, his mouth working as he tried to find the words, new tears springing to hurt eyes. His voice dipped low with shame as he forced the sentence out. "I hit her. I couldn't believe I had stooped so low.

"We decided then and there that we needed help, not only to find you, but also to find ourselves. We went to counselors and psychologists. No one could explain it all…or stop the pain and anger. Then one day, I met a man at work. He wasn't any more special than anyone else, but there was something different about the way he viewed life. He was new to the job. He worked on the roof truss crew.

"Not long after he started, he fell. He had been carrying a load of shingles across the roof. The pitch wasn't that steep and he had the proper footgear on, but something caused his foot to slip. If he hadn't been carrying the shingles, he probably could've righted himself, but they threw him too far off balance and he slid off the roof.

"It was quite a drop, but the strangest thing happened. It was like someone caught him in mid-air and cushioned his fall so that he didn't break a single bone or damage anything internally. One of the younger guys was working a table saw below him, and he landed on the table and it cut his hand off. Clean off. It fell into the sawdust and no one thought to get it when they rushed him to the hospital. It destroyed any chance of reattaching the hand.

"The first thing that went through my mind as I watched it happen was that he should have died, so someone must be watching out for him. The second was that the same someone had allowed him to lose his hand in the process, and I couldn't help but wonder why.

"It's pretty hard to do carpentry with no hand. The boss was good to him, though. He found things for him to do so he could keep his job. It would've destroyed anyone else. I'll never forget his words when I went to see him in the hospital. He just looked at me and said, 'Angus, don't worry about it. God's got something bigger for me. I don't know what it is, but he does, so I'll just wait for him to let me know.'

"I couldn't believe the man's faith in someone he couldn't even see. He didn't—not for a moment—doubt that God was in control of every part of the situation. I wanted that kind of faith so badly, so I found excuses to visit him, hoping he'd tell me more about this God of his.

"I asked the most difficult questions a man can ask, but I respected his answers because his faith never wavered. For months after the accident, I pestered him, challenging his God and struggling with the idea of believing blindly. Eventually he invited your mother and I to church, offering to drive us there the first few times, and we haven't stopped going since. He once told me that he thanked God for taking his hand because it allowed me to see the Lord at work.

"It took me a year to understand what it really meant to be a follower of Christ, but once I figured it out, I was on my knees in a minute."

Heather looked baffled.

"What do you mean, 'what it really meant to be a follower of Christ?' I thought we were Christians because we were born in a Christian country and lived a good life and tried to be nice to people. You mean there's more?"

Her father nodded, warming to the subject.

"As I said, it took me a year to 'get it.' So many people think that if they go to church, get baptized, give money, take communion, and behave morally, they're Christians. But the Bible, the very book they carry to church and read from on Sundays, says, 'All have sinned and fall short of God's glory.' I didn't realize that it wasn't about what I could do for God; it was what he had already done for me. Again, the Bible says, 'It is by grace you are saved, through faith, not of yourselves, it is the gift of God—not by works so no man can boast.'

"I had to understand that God didn't want my good deeds—he wanted my heart. He wanted me to see that I couldn't do anything with my life that would please him other than give it to him so he could fix it. That's why he came to earth in human form. He needed to experience the temptations and difficulties we face so he could understand and raise us above them. He died—separated himself from the perfection of Heaven—so we wouldn't have to be separated from him forever in Hell. And he rose from the dead to show that even death had no power over him. That's why Cyrus' scripture reading and our prayers had an effect on the evil spirit in you. The thing couldn't stand up against the all-consuming power of Christ."

Heather held up a hand at that point, eager to clarify what he was trying to tell her.

"What do you mean, 'evil spirit?' Was that what that thing was?"

Angus pulled his chair close and took Heather's small hand in his own massive one, absently tracing the dirt-caked nails.

"Yes, my sweet daughter, that's what that thing was. You'll understand better as you hear the rest of my story. As your mother and I continued learning about Jesus' love for us, we also started learning about a certain babysitter we had hired. Do you remember Cathy Tremble?"

Heather scrunched her nose in concentration. That was such a long time ago. Centuries, it seemed. And then a face floated before her mind's eye and she remembered a girl with plain brown hair, immaculately dressed in a dark blouse and skirt, sporting a discreet tattoo on her shoulder, and she nodded at the vague memory.

Heather recalled the tattoo with a slight shudder. It was a pentagon with a five-pointed star inside. A serpent coiled in and around the star. It was all in black and not much bigger than a coin. Cathy had waited until they were alone and pulled her sleeve off of her shoulder to show Heather, making the child promise not to mention it to anyone. She remembered tracing the design on impulse, unable to withdraw her hand until the older girl gently set it aside and covered her shoulder once more.

"We found out not long after we started going to church that she was heavily into some bizarre and remote form of Satan worship." Angus raked his fingers through sparse red and gray hair and heaved a burdened sigh, his heavy jaw twitching with the repeated struggle to let the anger go. "It's times like this when I wish we had taken you children to church and paid more attention to the Bible."

Heather watched him, curiosity and spiritual hunger begging her to listen closely as the tale continued unravelling before her.

"God's most beautiful angel, Lucifer, grew proud and rebellious. Because of that, God kicked him out of Heaven and called him Satan. He's the reason Adam and Eve were tempted in the Garden of Eden. He's the reason mankind is tempted at all. And he's the reason you had that monster in you.

"Cathy Tremble was at quite a high level in her particular coven or band. No one knew at the time that such a nice young lady was so willing to baby-sit because it gave her opportunities to use the innocence of children for her benefit.

After you disappeared, investigations revealed a few very nasty surprises. Some of the older children in the neighbourhood came forward to accuse Cathy of kidnapping you. It seems that she was notorious for taking children to meetings where they were prayed over and abused." Angus' voice failed him and his jaw muscles worked while he tried again to gain control of himself. He looked as though he would be sick, but pulled himself together, forcing the words through teeth clenched with loathing and disgust.

"We were so blind to it all, living in our own little world, not needing anything or anyone but ourselves. What a joke. A pathetically sick joke."

Heather looked at him in a strange pity, her heart heavy with remembrances. She could see the dark place. She didn't know where they had gone, but yes, she remembered holding Cathy's hand and walking with her into the blackened room. There were candles lit everywhere and people in dark robes were singing in a funny monotone way. She recalled feeling the cold and dampness of the place and she shivered involuntarily.

She was placed on a table and was given a candy to chew by a man who spoke in a soft and gentle voice. Cathy promised her more candy if she laid back and stayed still and just answered yes to any question asked. Heather recalled being afraid, but she had trusted Cathy and reluctantly agreed as she took the candy from the man and popped it into her small mouth.

Looking back, she realized that it wasn't a candy at all, but a sugar cube, and judging by the way her memory distorted the scenes that followed, it must have been laced with some kind of narcotic. She remembered the fear easing away and a strange detached feeling coming over her. At some point in her mind's recollections that same voice drifted through the haze and Heather shuddered anew at how close she had come to being violated.

"Can we take this one? She's quite small but very innocent. It would be good to become one with her. We could gain more power with one so young and pure."

Cathy had refused, stepping between her and the man who had spoken, and for a moment, Heather felt a twinge of gratitude toward her caregiver.

"You don't want her for that, Rusty. She's got a temper. She wouldn't stay passive for long and she can fight. Even in her suspended state, I think she would be more than we could handle right now. No, I think this one is a better offering to the lord himself. The anger is so close to her that it wouldn't take much for him to enter her. She is more suited to becoming one with lord Satan than with you, although I do understand that you enjoy them young. Maybe I'll bring Sarah to you again. She seems to enjoy it. And the drug doesn't seem to hurt her any. She becomes quite willing. What do you think?"

Heather almost retched with the recollection. She was only four and the man had talked of raping her. She looked at her father with doe-eyes and shook her head, trying to clear the evil from her mind but not succeeding.

"I remember. They thought I was too young. It's ok, Dad. No one hurt me. But they did pray over me. I remember. They chanted some stuff and bribed me to say 'yes' when they asked me stuff. They talked about lord Satan filling this vessel—that was me wasn't it? There was a lot of other stuff they said but I can't recall it. The man wanted me but Cathy offered some girl named Sarah instead."

Angus nodded, his voice hoarse with the emotions that roiled just below the surface.

"Yes, Sarah Kochenko. A brave girl, that one. She's the reason it all stopped. She's the one who stepped forward and accused Cathy of kidnapping. She was seventeen when you disappeared, and without her, no one would have ever known about the abuse. They had used her for their little ceremonies from when she was five until she no longer needed a babysitter. She went through a tremendous amount of therapy trying to get her life back together." Anger filled Angus' face as he continued on.

"Of course, all the members of the cult denied any knowledge of the girl, but she knew intimate things about them—things that a person could only know if they had seen them unclothed. Her sisters were interviewed separately. The authorities had little doubt they were telling the truth, so closely did the details of their stories match. The doctors examined Sarah and her three younger sisters and found not only had they been raped repeatedly, but they had all contracted syphilis. The cretins had given a sexually transmitted disease to little children.

"Once the brave girl stepped forward, others did as well. There were quite a number of families who had trusted sweet, gentle, wicked Cathy. About ten in all. It didn't take long for the children to lead the authorities to an old abandoned school in the industrial district. The windows had been boarded up and it looked unused—until they went inside.

"They found an altar—an old kitchen table—and candles set up around the room. A pentagon had been spray painted on the floor around the table and a bunch of old choir gowns had been modified and hung on some nails on the wall. There were handcuffs and a number of other nasty things. And enough of the children's hair and fluid samples were found, mixed with the same from several of the accused adults, that it was a pretty airtight case. The police tore their meeting place apart looking for you. Cathy and her crew were arrested for rape, child abuse…all sorts of stuff. But there was no sign of you there. You were still missing and we were still lost without you.

"By then, your mother had placed her trust completely in Jesus and told me not to give up hope. She knew you were still alive—how, I'll never know—and had faith that God would bring you back to us some day. I think that was probably around the time I started realizing what faith was all about. Your mother's example of blind trust drew me to the point where I was so envious that I wanted what she had. I placed my life, my fears and doubts—and you—in Christ's hands and felt peace and hope for the first time in my life."

Heather nodded slowly and stared at a crack in the dull tile floor, trying to absorb all she had been told. Angus took a sip of water from the glass that he had grabbed on his way through the kitchen, and cleared his throat, continuing with his own journey through the painful past.

"It didn't take me long to realize that God wanted me to tell our story, but I felt so inadequate. I wasn't a well-educated man and didn't think I would do a good job. I prayed about it constantly, asking God to show me what He wanted me to do and how to do it, and I began to study the Bible. Again, God used your mother to prod me in the right direction.

"I remember her coming into the bedroom one night while I was sitting up in bed reading from the book of Romans. I think she could feel my frustration and just blurted out her suggestion. 'Why don't you go to Bible College, Angus? You'd learn a whole lot more and you might discover what, exactly, it is that God wants you to do. The kids are all in school so I can take on a job during the day. The computer courses I took should help me get something decent. Think about it.' She climbed into bed, kissed my cheek, and rolled over to sleep. It all rang so true that I couldn't help but know it was the right path to take.

"I asked Jane about it again at breakfast the next day and she said that if she applied for a job and got it and I applied for college and got it, we would trust that to be God's answer. She had a job within a week and I was signed up for the next semester at Bible College.

"I worked hard, taking as many courses as I could. I studied about the occult and how it affected our world with you in mind. I got involved in a homeless shelter in London with your mother, and once I completed college, we, as a family, applied for a pastorate at a church here in Toronto. I couldn't believe how many people are held in bondage by the evil one and his demons. Not just street people either.

"We got involved with the group of clerics from across the city that ran Christ's Mercy and jumped at the chance when asked to come and join the work here. I was amazed at how smoothly it ran as a non-denominational shelter. I'm a Baptist pastor, there's a Pentecostal, a Presbyterian, a Catholic Priest—and I think an Anglican minister is joining us within the month.

"It isn't always easy working together because our doctrines can be quite different, but the men who work here believe that salvation comes through faith in Jesus Christ alone and that the Bible is the unchanging word of God. We believe in Jesus' life on earth, His death and His resurrection and that without Him, we can do nothing. As long as we all remember these things, we all get along fine. Beyond that, we try hard to agree to disagree."

Angus stopped, his face filling with emotion again, his words tight with a mix of joy and excitement, laced with tears and pain.

"And then you came through those doors on the back of a vagrant who cared about you and my world has tilted. Your mother will be beside herself with joy."

"She's here, in Toronto?" Excitement leapt to life in Heather's heart.

"Yep, and Fee as well."

"What about George?"

A momentary silence dampened the enthusiasm in the room, and Angus dropped his eyes to the floor.

"He didn't take your leaving well at all. He rebelled. I guess he blamed himself. He dropped out of high school and disappeared. Said this religious crap was just delusional garbage and that you were dead and we should all just accept it and get on with life. He would avoid us for months at a time. He'd take on work for a while and then travel. We'd get a note from time to time telling us where he was, but it was like he was always running away. I haven't seen him for almost a year now. It's hard to track him down. We keep praying. If only he could see you now. He'd certainly change his tune about God's ability to hear and answer prayer."

Heather sat for quite some time, numbed by all she'd been told. So much of her life with her family had been missed and it saddened her. So much evil had been let loose through her, changing lives and destinies for good and for bad, and she felt a heaviness settle in her chest. Charlie cleared his throat from across the table and pushed his open Bible toward her with a firm resolve.

"Heather, you'd better read this before we go any further. There's still an important decision you need to make and this will explain why." A look passed between father and son and Angus reached for the Book, setting it before Heather and pointing to the passage Charlie referred to, asking her to read it aloud to them.

"Luke 11:24," she began in a quiet voice, "When an evil spirit comes out of a man, it goes through arid places seeking rest and does not find it. Then it says, 'I will return to the house I left.' When it arrives, it finds the house swept clean and put in order. Then it goes and takes seven other spirits more wicked than itself, and they go in and live there. And the final condition of that man is worse than the first."

Heather set the Book down, hands trembling, and looked from one concerned face to another.

"What does this mean? Are you telling me that this thing could come back inside me and bring seven others with it?"

Both heads nodded, concern etched deeply on their faces. Heather looked back down at the book with unseeing eyes, her mind churning with an instant panic as memories of her years of bondage surged to the forefront of her thoughts. As far as she was concerned, there wasn't much of a choice.

"What do I do?"

Angus remained silent, allowing Charlie to gently lead his sister toward the Saviour. In his heart Angus rejoiced, knowing that, like himself, God was thrilled with the return of a wandering child. He marvelled as he watched his son, no longer the little boy he remembered, gently instructing Heather with a wisdom beyond his twenty years.

"Romans 10:9 says 'that if you confess with your mouth, "Jesus is Lord," and believe in your heart that God raised him from the dead, you will be saved. For it is with your heart that you believe and are justified, and it is with your mouth that you confess and are saved.'

"Heather, I can't do it for you. You have to believe in your heart all the Bible says about Jesus. You have to believe that He came, died, and rose again for you because he loves you. You have to have faith that He will take you to Heaven when you die simply because He said so and you have to tell Him about your belief. You have to recognize that He is far greater than the evil spirit that was in you and that He will never let it possess you again. We can't do that for you."

She understood, but felt suddenly shy. How could she approach the Creator of the world when she was so dirty inside? She had already met the incredible person Charlie called Jesus. She suddenly recognized that. He had been there, restraining the demon within her, and had taken her in his arms to lead her past it as it had been forced to run from the holy presence of God. She knew the purity and power, the strength and unfathomable love, and was aware of her imperfections and failures, afraid they would keep her from being acceptable. She voiced her concerns and her brother was quick to jump on them.

"Don't think any one of us is perfect, Heather. If I offered you a glass of water and then put a drop of poison in it while you watched—would you drink it?" She shook her head, a slight smile hovering on her mouth.

"Heaven's like that. Not one lie or evil thought is permitted before the presence of God. That means none of us qualify because that one sin would taint His presence like the poison tainted the water. He can't allow that, so He sent Jesus to absorb the poison in us, making us clean before Him. When God looks at us, He sees Jesus—if we have placed our lives in His hands.

"We still screw up, but we are forgiven constantly. God sees Jesus…not the sin that He died for. You aren't worthy, Heather—but neither am I. It's Christ who makes us worthy by faith. We simply believe and trust Him to take full and complete control of our lives, knowing that He will direct us far more capably than we can ourselves. And only you can make the choice that will allow Him to do that."

Heather looked at the ceiling but instead saw into her own heart. She saw the pain and wickedness, the loneliness and fear, and she released it all, crying out to her Saviour for forgiveness and redemption. She emptied herself before God and welcomed Him into a heart that began to beat the moment He touched it. And then she experienced the full force of His love for the first time. It was overwhelming, calming, soothing —incredible.

Somewhere in the spiritual world an evil spirit screamed in anguish at the loss of a soul. But all through the Heavenly realms, angels lifted their voices in song with a fervour and excitement, a joy and eagerness at the finding of a soul—Heather's soul.

Eight

BREAKFAST WAS OVER AND CLEARED AWAY, leaving several satisfied customers. The various mismatched couches and chairs were peopled with those concerned with the task of digestion in the brief time they had left before wandering off to their various jobs and duties. Heather was among them, groaning with the gratification that comes from eating too much of a delightful meal.

She chatted pleasantly with her friends but her mind was elsewhere. Thanksgiving day had arrived in the small community, and its residents were about to partake in a flurry of activity surrounding food and accommodation preparation. The tourist season was experiencing a lull and that was a good thing for those who belonged to the halfway house known as "Christ's Redeemed."

Looking back over the previous summer, Heather acknowledged that they had all been over-busy with the children's camps and the various tours run by the residents in the home. She was proud of the accomplishments met and surpassed by the mission's offshoot facility. Not only was it running debt-free, but it was providing jobs and a new life to those who sought help through Christ's Mercy in Toronto.

She glanced around the room, noting the weariness etched in the different faces. The season had been long and challenging, but rewarding in so many ways. Street children had been able to see a glimpse of what life could be. Through Christ's Redeemed camps, they were learning life skills and abilities in hopes that they would, later on, choose to leave the streets.

Heather and the others were grateful for the break they needed before the snow buried them and their winter snowmobile camps and tours took over. The brief time of rest allowed them to pour their rejuvenating energies into the

Thanksgiving preparations—and they all had so much to be thankful for.

She shook her head in wonder at God's abundant provision for all who had chosen the new life at Christ's Redeemed. They were approaching their second year running and were already talking about expansion. That meant more homeless people would finally find a place where they were wanted, respected and valued; a place where they could leave the ghosts of the past behind and where they could take pride in accomplishment and grow in faith.

The same photo that had once sat in the living room in her home in London graced the wall in the great room where she and the others lounged. Not for the first time, Heather soaked in each detail of each face as it smiled out upon the room. The wild and haunted expression in her eyes had become a reminder of God's power and mercy, and on those nights when the evil one approached, calling to her, she found her way to that photo and stared at it, thanking God for all He had done.

Turning away from the past's reminder, she purposefully headed toward the kitchen. She was eagerly looking forward to seeing her family again and had all sorts of culinary treats planned for them. It had been too long since their last gathering together. A tingling of excitement raced through her and she turned her mind back yet again.

Chapter Eight...

Reunions

HILDY WASN'T EXACTLY PLIABLE and warm at first. As a matter of fact, she had bordered on hostility, so deep was her fear of losing her friend. She had turned on Cyrus with a viciousness that surprised him, accusations thick and cruel, but Jimmy understood and just wrapped her in a gentle embrace. It was unexpected, and the middle-aged woman's defences crumbled completely as she surrendered to the feeling of security he offered, her forehead dropping against the firm chest as the tears spilled past her thick long lashes.

That was how Heather found the small group, and she wasn't sure her shocked system could stand any more.

"Well knock me over with a feather!"

Immediately, the two jumped apart, Jimmy knocking over a chair. Shorty chuckled as the guilty expressions spread across the dirty faces and Cyrus looked the other way, a discreet smile hidden within the folds of his peppered beard.

"It wasn't what you think. Tell her, Cyrus. I was just upset and Jimmy was giving me a hug. That's all." The words tumbled out of Hildy in a flustered stream as her cheeks reddened and she lifted her chin, a challenge glinting in her hazel eyes. No one offered a reply, so she took the opportunity to change the subject.

"So, where've you been?" Her voice was gruffer than she had wanted and she instantly regretted it as she saw Heather's smile waver uncertainly. She waved a hand in the air dismissively and tried again.

"Tell me all about it. I imagine you all have quite a tale, huh?"

Heather looked from her father to her brother and the light danced in her eyes as she repeated the story, adding her part of it for her family's benefit. Each of the vagabonds' reactions was different as the story unfolded. Shorty ignored it all for the most part, primping and patting her little mongrel as though there was no one else in the room. Hildy remained skeptical, but was willing to listen until it was finished. Cyrus nodded continually throughout the narrative, adding "amen's" and "halleluiahs" liberally. It was Jimmy who responded in the most unusual way of all.

The one-eyed man soaked in each word, savouring it for truthfulness, nodding thoughtfully, and upon the finishing of the tale he immediately pulled his chair back, dropped to his knees and spoke aloud, a shocked silence accompanying his words.

"God of these men—and Heather. Please hear me now. I've experienced your power first-hand now and I believe in you. I've lived on both sides of the street. You know, God, that I had money, and that I know it doesn't satisfy. You know I've lived with nothing and that doesn't bring true happiness either. God, I'm tired of searching high and low for something to fill my empty life. I'm ready for you to fill it and now I've seen that you can. I'm yours to do with whatever you want."

It was all said and done with a quiet firmness, and no one moved for fear of disturbing the atmosphere created by the prayer of complete faith. Heather smiled and then went to him, dropping to her knees beside him as she draped her arms across his shoulders in an embrace of joy.

Hildy gaped at her long-time friend as he continued to kneel in total surrender before the God of all creation—eyes squeezed shut and a look of such peace plastered all over his upturned face. As if her heart hadn't faced enough, and now this! She began to wail in despair, clapping her hands over a face filled with insecurity and anxiety. She wanted what they had but she still didn't understand it. What would God want with the daughter of a whore?

Angus watched her shrewdly, seeing her heart's words written in the expression on her face, and he stepped across the room to her, placing a hand on her arm. Violently, the woman slapped at it, angry that her world was shifting so abruptly. Through heaving gasps, she lashed out.

"This is all easy for you people. You've all come from good places. You, Cyrus, even you had a family and a job once…and you, Jimmy…how could you? You know I'm street trash and always have been. You lived a good life once…all of you, but I'm nothing. I'm worth nothing!"

Her voice rose in anguish as she stumbled toward the door, and this time Heather went to her.

"Hildy, stop for a minute and look at me. Haven't you heard what I told you? I was a vessel for God's ultimate enemy. If anyone should be rejected, don't you think it would be me?" Hildy stopped just before the door, the plea reaching some place in her heart and mind.

"Maybe God chose this time and place just so you could see how much love He has for you. You've been such a great friend to me for these past seven years. I know you wanted that wicked thing taken from me. You loved and nursed me after it had its way. God answered prayers that you didn't even realize you were praying. If He was willing to reach into my soul and rescue me from Satan himself, don't you think He would overlook your past?"

Heather approached her friend and wiped at the fat drops that coursed through the dirt on Hildy's cheeks, a new and formidable love shining through the younger woman's eyes.

"I know what it's like to feel unworthy, Hildy. You of all people know how much evil was in me. I know how desperate you feel. Remember that I was there only a few hours ago. I'm free, Hildy. Cyrus didn't hurt me; he helped me. Jimmy sees that and has just wanted the same thing I have. I want that for you. Let us help you."

Hildy shook her head fiercely. It was too frightening and too much for her to understand at that time. She pushed herself away from the gentle hands and turned her back again, wrapping her arms around herself in despair. Heather sighed deeply and shrugged.

"Then at least don't leave us. You've been like a mother to me. Don't leave me now, Hildy." She stared openly at the woman's back, silently pleading, praying for her friend's lost soul.

Hildy nodded with reluctance and tightly controlled relief. She was still wanted and that was worth more than any of them would realize. She could deal with this Christian stuff later. For now, Heather was right. It was a good thing that the monster was gone. So what if Jimmy got religious. It sure hadn't hurt Cyrus any. In the meantime, Heather needed her here and here was where she'd stay. Squaring her shoulders, she nodded again, and turning, gave her young friend a firm hug, clinging longer than she ordinarily would.

* * *

The clergy were generous to the small group, encouraging them to stay at the shelter for the night. Each vagrant was kindly presented with a variety of new articles—a bar of soap, a towel and a clean change of clothes. Each took turns using the shower facilities, washing away years of dirt and grime, scrubbing themselves free of all that would mark them as belonging to the street. Sparks of hope and uncertainty flickered within the hearts of the small group, teasing each person with the hint of a better life, struggling against the well-established attitude of worthlessness and defeat, and they all felt beyond their depth as they prepared to meet for the evening meal in the common room.

It was strange to them all, sitting at the table with the clerics, clean and tidy, while people they had mingled with on the street earlier that day sat a short distance away, still grubby and destitute. It amazed them that so few of those acquaintances recognized them—or perhaps they chose not to—and the small group felt more than a little uneasy.

On several occasions, Heather intercepted covert glances from Hildy as the woman eyed a cleaner, more attractive Jimmy. Her face wore a baffled expression and she blushed to the roots of her hair when Jimmy caught her stare with his own bashful glance. On one level, Heather listened as her father and brother retold their twenty-one-year-old story to the other clergy around the table. At another level, she studied the game of eye tag played not very subtly by her two friends, and was amazed that she had been with them for so many years and hadn't seen the obvious attraction.

Shorty had refused to be drawn into the strange group, choosing to sit in her same foul and worn clothing, still caked with dirt and grime, at the far end of the room with people she knew from the streets. Heather looked her way and caught the old woman staring back at her resentfully. She returned the hostile look with a questioning smile, hoping to draw the old woman back into the group. As she sat eating her portion, the shutters came down over the woman's face and her expression returned to one of daydream oblivion. Heather shivered nervously at the obvious anger displayed by the old woman. She looked at her for a moment longer and then turned back to the conversation at hand.

*   *   *

Nothing can come close to explaining the feeling that comes over a woman when her child, who was once lost to her, is finally returned. Jane went numb with shock as the words tumbled through the telephone into her ear, not quite registering in her brain. At first she was certain it was an evil prank, then a mistake, and then she acknowledged it for the truth that it was and let out a reflexive squeal. Without explanation to her coworkers, she grabbed her purse and keys, knocking her chair askew, and bolted for the door.

The normally placid native woman never once eased up on the old car's accelerator, stopping only long enough to pick up her youngest daughter from the high school she was attending. Nothing was said during the drive to the mission other than to repeat the bare essentials revealed over the telephone and to mutter impatiently at the drivers who obstructed her path. Through most of the drive both of the vehicle's occupants sat totally absorbed in memories from the past, not wanting to voice the fears that kept trying to surface above the excitement of seeing Heather again.

The traffic was brutal, slowing them to a crawl. A trip that should have taken no more than a half hour stretched out to cover a two-hour time span thanks to a mechanical failure in the truck that blocked the intersection ahead of them. Jane and Fee fretted constantly, praying that they would make it to the mission before it was too late, fearing that Heather would disappear onto the streets again before they had a chance to see her.

They parked their car haphazardly in the secure underground parking garage below the mission and raced the flight of stairs to the common room above, their hearts pounding with anticipation. And then they saw her.

In that moment, when their eyes met across the room, recognition was immediate and Jane forcefully shoved her way through throngs of protesting people to her oldest daughter, her gaze never leaving Heather's flushed and eager face. Fiona could only follow in shock, remembering her sister's appearance from a distant gap through time.

And then they were together, hugging, crying, touching each other's faces; and it was as though the lost seven years didn't exist. Heart-wrenching apologies passed back and forth, each trying to take responsibility for evil that wasn't theirs to be credited for. And then, finally, glory was given to the One who rightly deserved it when they realized that Heather had come home spiritually as well as physically.

Hildy was shy and self-conscious as she remembered her statement from earlier in the day about being a mother to Heather. She took a step back, trying to fade into the surroundings, but Heather turned, deliberately looking for her, grabbed her hand and pulled her forward to stand before the dark-haired beauty who was her biological mother. It was a little strange noticing for the first time that both women were around the same age, but Heather continued with her introduction in spite of the fleeting thought.

"Mom, I'd like you to meet my best friend, Hildy. She's been like a mom to me. She's protected me and cared for me for the past seven years. I couldn't have had a better friend if you had personally chosen her for me, and I know I wouldn't be alive today if it weren't for her." Hildy shrugged in embarrassment at the tribute.

Heather waited with a sudden uncertainty as she watched her mother stand perfectly still, eyeing her friend with a shuttered expression, wondering if she saw the tobacco stains on the woman's hands, the uneven and shaggy hairstyle, or the street craftiness in the depths of her eyes. And then Jane stepped forward, threw her arms around Hildy's shoulders, and clung to her gratefully, weeping freely as she thanked her daughter's friend.

"I owe you more than you know. You've been an answer to seven years of prayers. Thank you."

Jane released her as quickly as she had embraced her, a smile splitting her face, while Hildy stood and gawked in surprise, unsure of her next move. Her face coloured brightly and she dropped her eyes to gaze shyly at her feet, but secretly, she glowed with a warm pleasure at the welcome.

Jimmy and Cyrus were next to be introduced and Jane shook hands with them. Heather was pleasantly surprised to find that her family already knew Cyrus. He had been helping at the mission for quite some time, and was treated with respect by all. Shorty refused to budge from her seat at the crowded table near the food line when they gestured for her to come and be introduced. Instead, she acted as though she hadn't seen them and turned back to her plate of food, leaving Heather and Hildy to exchange concerned glances.

They celebrated that evening with a passion appreciated only by those who understand the bonds of true love and family and how fragile they can be. Food and merriment abounded in the smaller common room that connected the various offices and sleeping areas. The stories were told again, adding details that were missed in the first telling, and more praise was given to God for His kindness that day.

And then they settled down for the night, Heather and Hildy sleeping in the MacDonald's small apartment, Cyrus and Jimmy at the shelter. Heather, Hildy and Fiona talked late into the night, sharing all that had been missed in the past seven years until sleep finally claimed them.

*　　　*　　　*

The next day was a busy one, and full of surprises. Jimmy had left early that morning with the command that everyone—meaning the MacDonalds, the clergy, and Hildy, Cyrus and Shorty—were to meet him in the common room where they could discuss an idea he had. The man was clean and filled with purpose and didn't return until later that afternoon

The young police officer, David, had been invited as well, Jimmy telling himself that it didn't hurt to have someone who worked the legal side of the streets included. He was thrilled when the lad agreed, noticing the interest shown whenever Heather's name was brought into the conversation—not that Jimmy was inclined toward matchmaking at all.

The gathering of people talked quietly among themselves, with the exception of Shorty, who sat in a corner alone, stroking her dog thoughtfully. Everyone wondered where Jimmy had gone at such an early hour, fearing something was wrong or that he had regretted his decision to become a believer.

Promptly at two o'clock, he strode purposefully into the room, a suit decorating his lean frame and his bald head shining from a fresh shave. Under his arm was tucked a thick bundle of papers stuffed into a file folder, a pen clipped onto the stiff edge of the outer cover. This was a side to Jimmy that none of them had ever seen before and they all froze, staring at him in disbelief. Then Heather remembered his tale of being a business man in a high stress job and she could see the image of that past life in him now.

Hildy gawked at him as though he were a stranger, the colour rising up her neck and creeping its way across her face to her hairline. Heather could see the storm brewing and began to pray, silently but fervently, that her friend wouldn't do anything rash. She tossed a glance at David, raising her eyebrows and meaningfully nodding toward Hildy. The young man returned the nod as he, too, watched her agitation.

Jimmy set the folder and papers on the table with a purpose and waited patiently until he had everyone's attention. Clearing his throat, he scanned the room with his single green eye, the other covered, for the first time, with a black patch, giving him the rakish look of a pirate.

"I've called all of you to this meeting for a reason." There was a smattering of chuckles at his professional air but Jimmy ignored them and continued on.

"I know you all think I haven't lived much of a life, but I actually managed an investment firm once upon a time." Silence settled across the room and suddenly everyone was listening closely.

"I had a nervous breakdown and turned to the streets as a way to straighten myself out. I couldn't handle the constant stress of working in such a big organization at the time. I was a perfectionist to the point where it almost destroyed me. I was extremely good at my job—but not good enough to meet my own impossible standards. I was considered one of the best in the financial industry, knowing where and when to invest the firm's money. I earned them a lot and didn't stop at their money. I worked my own as well, amassing quite a fortune.

"I've never been married and didn't live a fancy life to start with, so I just kept dumping my money into investments and letting it grow. I've kept track of it from time to time just out of curiosity, and I've kept in touch with my lawyer and accountant, who, by the way, think I'm absolutely nuts." This brought chuckles again.

"I've enjoyed most of my life on the street for the freedom it gave me and…" he looked significantly at Hildy, "for the friends I've acquired. But now it's time for me to be of some service to the society that once sheltered me.

"It appears that I am quite wealthy. Since I have no need of it, I thought that maybe the mission would be interested in an off-branch program that rehabilitates those who wish to get off the streets. I've been running around like crazy all morning, driving my lawyer and accountant wild, and I've come across a great piece of property near a little village called Restoule, which is being purchased as we speak. It's way up in the boonies near North Bay, but it's got great fishing, boating, and swimming.

"The property stretches right down to the lake. It's a one-hundred-acre farm and my accountant was the previous owner. He's been more than willing to contact my lawyer and arrange a transfer of ownership for the right price. Now Christ's Mercy owns it if they want it. He informs me that it would make a great tourist center, offering camping in the summer and snowmobiling in the winter. I am also willing to donate the money necessary to build a facility that will house several people who have shown a willingness to be reintroduced into society but don't yet have the skills to be able to do so.

"So, what does everyone think?"

The silence was palpable, and more than one mouth hung open in disbelief.

Heather gaped from Jimmy to Hildy—who sat stunned with a wild look plastered to her face—to her father, and back. Angus was the first to react, jumping to his feet and offering a robust hand of applause.

"Who are we to refuse a gift from God? I can't speak for the other gentlemen around the table…" his nod indicated his fellow clerics, "but you have my vote if that's what you're looking for. We'll likely have to go through the paper work with the committee, but if all is as it seems, I can hardly wait to do this thing alongside of you, Jimmy."

Hildy rose and quietly left the room, followed closely by Shorty, who tisked none too quietly, muttering about people's secret lives. Only Heather noticed the light fade in Jimmy's eyes as he watched in disappointment while his good friends slipped away.

Later, when he was able to, Jimmy left the clerics to discuss the smaller details and went in search of his companions. It didn't take long for him to find them. They waited a mere block away, Shorty sifting through a garbage can and Hildy drawing heavily on a cigarette butt.

"I'm sorry, Hildy. I should've told you first." His shoulders slumped when she turned her back to him and took another drag. Suddenly the dark, pinstriped suit he had bought to impress her and the others felt heavy and garish, silly in its contrast from his clothing of the day before.

"I thought I knew you, Jimmy. I thought you were just like me. I knew you had lived in their world in the past but I didn't know that you were leading a double life. I just feel like my whole world is being torn out from under me. People I thought I knew aren't what they seem anymore. Look at you…so fancy and clean…like the people who pass us every day, ignoring us 'cause we're not good enough for them." Her voice grew tight with unshed tears and she exhaled smoke on a heart-heavy sigh. "I just don't want to be hurt."

Suddenly, arms gently surrounded the woman, turning her, and she was pulled against a firm, fresh smelling chest.

"Hildy, you mean so much to me. You always have. I've always been amazed at how you took the life you were handed and made it something better. I admired you for that. Me—I took the life I had and threw it away. Almost. I didn't want you to think that I thought I was better than you because I was still involved in my old life, so I never told you. I've loved you for years and was so afraid of losing you. I was wrong, though, wasn't I?"

With thumb and forefinger, he tipped her chin, raising her face and allowing him to search deeply into her eyes. He liked, very much, what he saw. Dropping his own clean-shaven face, he placed a soft and tender kiss on pouting lips, his heart warming as he felt the coldness of anger leave her.

Breaking away after a moment he lifted his gaze over the top of Hildy's head to catch sight of Shorty as she stood off to the side, a dreamy smile on her face, watching with great interest. He smiled at the old woman with fondness, winking as though they all shared a secret. Together, the three of them turned, knowing they had much to face, and headed back to the mission.

Nine

SHE HATED HOUSEKEEPING WITH A PASSION, but someone had to do it. Heather wrinkled her nose as she scrubbed around the toilet bowl. Disgusting job. She allowed her mind to drift again, not wanting to dwell on the task at hand.

It had been pure delight clearing up the dishes that morning and she chuckled as she thought about it. Heather had cleared the table while Hildy washed the dishes and Jimmy dried. Hildy had taken to housekeeping like a duck to water. She seemed to love it.

Sometimes it got a little sickening watching the two of them make calf eyes to each other, and that morning had been especially sappy. Heather had had pretty much all she could take of the love-life of the middle aged couple, and so had discreetly slipped her hand into the soapy dish water when Hildy wasn't looking and splashed the pair of them.

That was all it took to start the three-way water fight that soon became a riot as the rest of the residents joined in. Heather's smile weakened some as she thought of how much Shorty would have liked the fight. She missed the addled old girl, but that choice hadn't been hers to make, so she let the thought drift away as others took its place.

The water fight eliminated the need to mop the kitchen floor, Heather reflected with a smile, since most of the water ended up there and they had needed to wipe it up anyway. Perspective changes the way a person views anything, so she attempted to focus on a way to make bathroom-cleaning fun. She paused in her work to think of something. Nope. It was hopeless; she just couldn't imagine anything that would turn scrubbing toilets into a romantic moment.

Romantic moments. Now wait, there was a topic that could take her mind off of her present task!

Chapter Nine...

Let No Man Separate

JIMMY WAS PATIENT. Patient like no other man could be. He loved Hildy dearly. It was one of the main reasons he had stayed in the park for fifteen years. It was why he had been afraid to tell her of his accumulating wealth. It was why he decided not to change his lifestyle even after she knew.

He had changed from the severe new suit back to the same old red bandanna, faded denim jacket and jeans. The shabby and patched clothes had been scrubbed to within an inch of their life. Inside and out, Jimmy was clean and life couldn't be better—for the most part.

He sat on the park bench, looking out over what had been his home for so long, and smiled. He'd had a good life. There were parts of it that he wouldn't care to keep, like struggling to stay warm in the freezing weather, but he had loved the freedom and camaraderie of street life. There were terrifying times, too. He'd had his share of punk teens trying to rough him up for any money he might have on him. There were those who took pleasure in hurting the street people as a sport. He had learned to avoid their kind quickly. He was getting too old for street life, though. He wanted to settle down into a nice little home with the right woman. With Hildy.

He drew a strong breath in through his nose, savouring the familiar scents that wafted on the air. There was Bobby's "Sausage on a Bun" stand wafting out the spicy smell of Oktoberfest sausages. Mixed in was the tangy fragrance of cut grass and car exhaust, a bizarre contrast of nature and city, and he smiled with satisfaction, enjoying the moment.

He had been struggling over what to do about Hildy. She was so beautiful now. It wasn't just her looks, either. She had an incredible spirit of giving, a generous heart, and yet there was a firmness about her that kept her from giving in to an easier way of life. She could have followed her mother's path easily; she had the looks, but she had too much personal pride for that. She would rather starve than sell herself, and Jimmy adored her for that strength.

She wasn't a believer, though, and that was the core of his dissatisfaction. Angus had pulled Jimmy aside earlier to discuss their relationship and Jimmy wasn't sure if he was grateful or not. He thought back to the verse that the Scotsman had shown him. Something about not being unequally yoked. Jimmy sighed. But he wanted to be yoked to Hildy. He loved her. But he loved Christ, too. More. Again he sighed, took Angus' second piece of advice, and lifted his plea to Heaven.

"Lord, it's me again. I know I've already asked you about a hundred times, but Angus says you're never too busy to listen. I love Hildy. She's an incredible woman. I know she'd survive without me, but I don't want her to. I know you're all I really need and I'll trust you with my life, but I can hope it will be a life beside Hildy. Can you show her in some way that I only want what's best for her? Would you please open her heart so she can see your love through me? I can't stand the thought of her being held captive by the same kind of creatures who held Heather…and she is. She just doesn't know it. I want her to experience the same love, peace, and forgiveness that I have experienced. I want her to see that she is a valuable person just because you created her. I don't think I could love anyone else, Lord, so if you say 'No,' I'll just figure you want me to be alone. I love you, Lord, and I'm so grateful that you saw past the dirt and grime and garbage in my life and loved me anyway. Help me to keep strong in my faith. In Jesus' name."

He buried his head in his hands and sat like that for a few moments, unmoving. A sudden rustle in the grass behind him caused his head to whip around as he sat up. There stood Hildy, wide-eyed, frozen to the spot and cheeks flushed with embarrassment and shame.

"I didn't mean to listen in on your prayer, Jimmy."

Her voice was soft and uncertain—insecure.

"I came looking for you for supper. I thought you might be here after all that time inside. I'm…I'm…sorry I disturbed you." She hung her head, turning to leave.

Jimmy was beside her instantly, a restraining hand placed gently on her arm.

"Wait, Hildy. Can we talk?" The woman merely nodded and allowed him to turn her back toward the bench. He settled himself next to her, as close as he decently could, and took hold of her dainty hand.

"Hildy, I've really messed this whole thing up, haven't I? I've been telling Jesus how I feel but not sharing it with you—again. You would think I'd learn after the first time, wouldn't you? So I guess I'd better start now.

"Girl, I love you. But you already know that. As for overhearing my prayer—I'm glad you did. Maybe it'll make it easier for you to understand me when I say that for us to be a couple now wouldn't be a good thing. It would be unfair to you because you would try to be religious for my sake and you wouldn't be happy. But…" he held up his hand when she gasped, "I don't want anyone else but you.

"So I guess what I'm asking you to do is to ask questions. Try to find out why Cyrus, Heather and I have chosen the way we have. I will wait for you until I die, Hildy, but I won't put you into a relationship with expectations. I want you, but I'll wait until you understand what I've done and why I did it."

Part of Hildy wanted to be angry. It sure sounded like she was being dumped, and yet, as much as her heart knotted, her head told her that Jimmy made perfect sense. He had been very clear that he didn't want life together to be a burden on her, and she was wise enough to know that with him being religious and her fighting it, it would be. She looked up at him and nodded sadly.

"I'll try it your way, Jimmy. I care a lot about you, too, and I don't want to lose you even if we don't become more than friends. So…why did you do what you did?"

Jimmy looked up into the branches of the tree above him and pulled his thoughts together before answering. His voice was distant and controlled.

"All my life, I've been the skinny nerd. I was a perfectionist in all I did. My grades were top of the class. I graduated with first class honours in math. I excelled at everything I put my hand to, but it wasn't enough. Each time I looked at my own handiwork I saw the flaws—the imperfections—and I felt like a failure. Even here on the streets, I felt inadequate. I wasn't big and strong. I never knew the right things to say to make you like me more. Again, I felt like a failure. And then I saw Cyrus, Angus, and the others get that thing out of Heather and I finally understood the big picture. Heather didn't do anything to deserve God's intervention. She didn't have to be perfect at anything. She was His child and that was enough for Him. Your love for Heather is kind of the same. You didn't care about the evil spirit in her, did you?" He waited, watching her while she shook her head with conviction.

"You just wanted to help her because she needed it. When I realized that God didn't care how perfect my life was, it was like the sun coming out after a very long winter. That's why I'm not going to worry about what happens to you and me. If I let Jesus look after it, it'll work out the way it should. If I try to do it, I'll fail—again. Does any of that make sense?"

Hildy's head was bowed in thought and she nodded and smiled a weak smile.

"Yes, I think I understand a bit. I need to think about it all, though. Thanks for everything, Jimmy. I don't know what I'd do without you." She leaned over and placed a shy peck on Jimmy's smooth warm cheek, feeling his desire to respond within him as she did so. Rising from the bench, they turned, meandering in the direction of the mission in silence, each focusing on their own thoughts.

*   *   *

Hildy sat quietly at the table, pushing her food around on her plate, and Cyrus glanced uneasily her way a few times. It didn't take a rocket scientist to figure out that something was eating at that girl and he was going to find out what it was. He knew she would need to leave soon. She was from the streets, and street people were a breed unable to stay in buildings for long. She looked restless and would soon find a way to escape into the open night.

Sure enough, as soon as she was able, Hildy slipped quietly from the crowded cafeteria to the busy street out in front of the building. Cyrus followed discreetly until he caught up with her a block away.

"Nice night for a walk." His voice still held the gravelly rumble of years of street life but there was a new timbre to it. It carried concern and gentleness, and Hildy glanced sideways at the old man as he matched his shuffle to her own easy stride.

"Yah. It is." They walked on in silence for another block. Finally, Hildy could stand it no more and stopped, turning to Cyrus, who stopped with her.

"Can I ask you something, Cyrus?" He nodded willingly, his grizzled whiskers bobbling with the movement, and they returned to their stroll.

"Why did you get into this religion thing?" She sounded almost too casual as she queried, and Cyrus worked at restraining a knowing smile.

"How long have we known each other, Hildy?" The question caught her off guard and she shrugged.

"Probably since I was little."

"Yep, that's right. And in all that time have I ever cared about anyone but myself?"

She laughed a short bark and answered honestly.

"No."

"That's right—until I found out what Andy was doing to Heather. Something inside me kind of curled up and died when I realized what I'd done. But it was too late. I almost drank myself to death after that.

"Then one day, I ended up at the mission. Don't even ask me how I got there; I was so drunk. I just remember the Catholic feller saying that if he didn't know better he'd think I was trying to kill myself. Some of what he was saying actually soaked through my booze-fogged brain and I took a reality check. I was killing myself and didn't care. The reverends and such there did care, though. They sobered me up and started talking to me. I told them all the things I'd done and that I was pretty worthless, and they showed me in their Bibles where it said I wasn't worthless. They showed me stories of Jesus loving the beggars and the poor and I realized that if I had been there back then, He would've loved me, too.

"It wasn't hard for me to become a Christian man. It was hard giving up the booze though. I'd been at it so long, I didn't know if I'd live without it. It was some terrible living through those first few weeks, but Jesus came through it with me. Every time I was tempted, I turned to the story where the devil tempted Jesus, and I knew He understood. I left it in His hands each time and it just got easier and easier.

"Now I don't think my life would be much without Him. To be honest with you, I can't wait until Jimmy and Angus get going on this Christ's Redeemed place in the woods. I'm about ready to get out of this here city and live a quieter, safer life. You should go too, Hildy. I think you'd like it."

Hildy stopped dead in her tracks. Why hadn't she thought about them all leaving the city? They wouldn't want her to go. She wasn't religious like them. She wouldn't fit in. Cyrus could see the panic behind her distant stare and he laid a comforting hand on her shoulder.

"Don't even think it, Hildy. If you think Jimmy would leave you behind, you're a fool. That boy won't go anywhere without you. He'll pay for the place, and pay to keep it running, but wherever you are—that's where he'll be."

Hildy blushed at the observation, but Cyrus merely waved it aside.

"Tell you what, young lady. Why don't you test the Lord?"

She looked at him quizzically, cocking her head to the side.

"Just lay it before Jesus. Ask Him to show His love to you in some way. You know what your own heart is like inside, so why don't you challenge Him to love you? If He truly cares and wants you as His child, He'll answer."

"I'll think about it Cyrus…oh, and hey…thanks." She gave him a light kiss of gratitude on the cheek and headed down the street, leaving the old man standing, grinning foolishly, hand touching his newly kissed, crimson face.

* * *

"Jesus…God…whoever you are, I'm here. I feel kinda dumb standing out in the middle of nowhere in the middle of the night talking to the air, but I guess that's what's gotta be done, right?" She paused in the silence, ignoring the curious stares from three prostitutes gathered around the nearby light post as she tried to collect her thoughts.

Lifting her gaze to the night sky she noticed, for the first time, the vastness of the heavens, sparkling with the few stars visible in the overpowering light of the city park. A thought flitted through her mind, prodding her to recognize the greatness of the hand that created it all and still desired to know His creation personally. She shied away from that thought, intimidated by it, and continued in her monologue.

"I've asked the questions, like Jimmy said, and I think I understand it all, but I just don't see how someone so huge and important as you can love someone as worthless as me. Cyrus said I should test your love so that's what I'm gonna do.

"God, if you really love me and want me as your child, you are gonna have to show me that I'm needed. I've always been kind of the mother figure for the weak ones here in the park. Now with Jimmy trusting you and Heather and Cyrus too, there's just me and Shorty, and she's pretty independent and doesn't seem to want to have anything much to do with this whole religion thing. I guess you're just gonna have to do something pretty spectacular to make me see that you want me. I guess you probably know how badly I need to be needed. So I don't know what else to tell you, but, I guess, thanks for listening anyway."

Hildy shivered a little, feeling the unnerving presence of something or someone unseen, and pulled her jacket tighter around her to ward off the accompanying chill. Glancing one last time at the firmament above her, she turned and made her way back to the mission, tossing the occasional glance over her shoulder, her mind playing tricks with her, whispering to her that she was not alone.

Jimmy stood at the mission door, waiting anxiously for her return. He paced impatiently, taking a few steps toward the park, turning and repeating the action in the opposite direction. As she glided into the light of the single bulb hanging from the top of the doorway, he pounced, taking her hand firmly and half-dragging her into the building and toward the offices as he clipped off hurried sentences at her over his shoulder.

"Everyone's been waiting for you, Hildy. We had a meeting to decide who would be on the planning committee for Christ's Redeemed, and the Board wants to talk to you about it." While she sputtered in confusion, he continued to hustle her along, quickly guiding her through the double doors that separated the dining area from the section where the offices were housed. The doors whispered shut behind the two, leaving behind the curious stares of the few who loitered in the half-empty cafeteria.

"Why me? What do I know?" She almost whined the question, apprehension building in her as he continued to prod her on.

The men rose to their feet as Jimmy and Hildy entered the warm and stuffy room, and she blushed for the second time that day. Heather caught her eye and winked mischievously, receiving raised eyebrows in reply. Angus was the first to speak as they all seated themselves again, and his words were directed to the flustered street woman.

"Hildy, we've all been talking about the new facility and what is needed to run it. We all thought of you. You've lived on the streets all your life, giving you a special understanding into a way of thinking and doing things that none of us could understand. Charlie has agreed to oversee the place, but we need someone to be a kind of den mother for the women. Jimmy has made it very plain that if you are willing he will hold an equal position of responsibility over the men and, at the very least, will look after the business end of it. Heather will be there, as well, organizing the camps.

"We really felt that you would be the perfect one. You know what street life is all about. You know who's scamming and who's sincere. You have the leadership qualities that we need. We'll assign a different cleric and his family to stay at the facility each month to deal with the spiritual guidance needed. And you won't have to worry about finances, thanks to Jimmy's generosity. This would actually be a paying job. We trust your character and strength to do the job adequately. If, after a couple of months, you don't want to continue, we will try to find someone else, but we really think you're a perfect fit for the job. What do you think?"

Hildy sat there dumbly, thunderstruck over the turn of events. If she had any doubts about there being a God who cared, they were gone. She rose unsteadily and cleared her throat. Her voice wavered as she attempted to reply.

"Thank you for thinking of me. I have to think about it, and there is something I need to do first. Can I give you an answer tomorrow?" She was relieved when they all nodded, and then she bolted from the room, leaving them to stare at the door as it drifted closed behind her.

Back in her small cubicle, Hildy wasted no time and sat on her bed, head in hands, pouring out her heart to God, amazed at His quick answer.

"Well, God, I guess you must love me. I sure didn't expect you to answer that fast, and I would have never thought it would be like that. I don't know if I'm able to do this big job. I've never had one before, what with living on the streets. I wouldn't know where to begin. I guess that's what trusting you must mean, huh? So I give it all to you, like everyone said I should. I gotta believe that you'll show me how to do things right. Thanks so much. I've never been loved like this before and I never thought I could be…" her voice failed her as love welled up in her soul, so great it threatened to swallow her as it overtook her.

Time ceased to exist as the vagabond felt the chains of bondage drop from her heart, and her loving heavenly Father swept her up in an embrace of such magnitude that she was content to stay there indefinitely. Doubts and heartache seeped away, leaving her filled with eternal peace.

Opening her eyes, lashes clustered with salty tears, Hildy looked around her small cubicle with a new awareness, seeing, for the first time, the love and care expressed through each donated piece of furniture or necessity, and realizing the amazing Person who prompted such generosity. After that small span of time, she was certain of her path as she rose from the cot and headed out the door.

None were prepared for her take-charge attitude as Hildy burst through the office door resolutely and announced in her firm voice,

"Yes! Yes, I'll do it."

Jimmy's eyes began to dance as he saw that the very miracle he had been praying for had taken place in Hildy's heart. Just by the contentment that shone on her lovely face, he could sense the change even before anything could be said. He rose from his place at the table, stepped to her, and wrapped her in a tight hug, ignoring her embarrassment and the awkward looks thrown their way by those present.

"Welcome to the family," he whispered gently in her ear, and she replied with a squeeze and a light grin. Heather approached the couple curiously, unsure of what had just happened, but when Hildy turned to her, eyes shining with the unearthly light that comes from the rebirth of a soul, Heather let out a small whoop of joy and joined in on the hug.

* * *

The planning of Christ's Redemption quickly moved into the building stages, and everyone worked with a happy heart—all, except Shorty. She resented the changes that were taking place. She was comfortable in her little world and had no intention of leaving it. With that in mind, she bundled up her small dog and disappeared into the anonymity of the streets.

Had she known how they mourned her, she might have changed her mind about leaving. The few in the mission who cared for her cried over the emptiness her absence created. Many prayers were offered up for the protection and deliverance of the sweet and addled little old lady known as Shorty.

Life moved on, and with it came more changes. Heather, Hildy, Jimmy and Cyrus spent much time together studying the scriptures and learning new skills that would help them with the work in the north. Jane was a patient woman, teaching both ladies basic manners and domestic skills. Father Michael was a wiz with computers and went out of his way to teach Jimmy how to step into the modern world of finance, amazed by his ability to learn quickly. Angus shared his carpentry talents with the wealthy hobo, mixed with much common sense knowledge gleaned from his years on the farm. Charlie, an apprenticing electrician, worked with Cyrus, showing him the foundation of proper wiring and circuitry work. Each of them fought the complacency they had lived with, striving to master all that was placed before them in preparation for the ministry they all were to share. Some days were a celebration of their accomplishments. Other days brought them frustration and anger—and then repentance.

Hildy and Jimmy were masters at sifting through the vagrant society and picking out those who really wanted a new start, and it wasn't long before a dozen men and women of all ages were working alongside them, learning new skills and eagerly waiting for the day when they could leave the streets and begin again.

Heather noticed, with happiness, the blooming relationship between her two friends, and wasn't surprised at all when they stood one evening after a particularly delightful meal, waiting patiently to be noticed over the commotion in the room. One by one, voices quieted and all eyes turned to the red-faced couple as they shuffled awkwardly in the silence. Finally, Jimmy looked around the room at those he now considered family and cleared his throat nervously.

"Hildy and I have an announcement to make. It appears that this beautiful and amazing woman standing beside me has taken leave of her senses and consented to marry me." Chuckles peppered the air, intermingled with gasps of surprise and delight, and he held up his hand to continue.

"I've never been in this kind of situation before, but I have to say that God is blessing my socks off by giving me Hildy…and since neither of us has any idea how this whole wedding thing is done, we'll need plenty of advice and helping hands."

A hearty round of applause accompanied the announcement, followed by hugs and back slaps all around. Heather's heart nearly burst with excitement as she turned to look at David, wanting to share her joy with someone. She was surprised to find that he was already watching her with eyes as bright blue as her brother's, unexplainable emotions roiling in their depths. And then the shutters closed, sealing off the window to his soul as he smiled back at her, the serious expression changing to one of camaraderie.

Heather's brow wrinkled slightly as uneasiness settled upon her, and her smile wavered. He was an attractive man, kind to a fault, and always willing to offer a hand when he felt she needed it. Why did she feel so awkward, then, when he came near? He had never done anything inappropriate, and when she approached her mother about it, Jane, her eyes twinkling mischievously, had reassured her of the man's integrity and then left her daughter to wonder about the sly expression she was unable to hide.

Shrugging mentally, Heather turned her attention back to her friends, rising to join in the congratulations. Embracing them firmly, she almost pounced in her excitement.

"When did you guys decide on this?"

"It's been a long time coming," was all Jimmy would say as he kissed his bride-to-be on the forehead.

* * *

Heather stood in her sister Fiona's bedroom staring in awe at her friend, Hildy, as the older woman looked soberly through the window that opened onto the noisy street in the heart of the city. The woman's short brown hair swirled and twisted in a masterpiece of curls around a lovely face lightly dusted in muted tones of makeup. Her dress was knee length and pink, defying the traditional white of a bride's gown. Jimmy had wanted to find her the best wedding gown money could buy, but Hildy would have none of that. As it was, she knew she would find it difficult to adjust to her new life and didn't need the additional stress of pomp and ceremony.

Large hazel eyes stared intensely at the scenes below her. Cars and trucks honked, engines revving, and people laughed and yelled back and forth at each other. A jackhammer pounded thunderously against a partitioned-off section of the pavement. Hawkers and con artists peddled their wares to any and all that passed their way. Hildy saw none of it, so intense was her introspection. It took Heather's light touch on her arm to bring her out of her thoughts, and she turned to her maid of honour.

"What if he changes his mind, Heather? What if he doesn't show up? I don't think I could face that."

The younger girl smiled in understanding and shook her own cluster of carefully arranged curls in response.

"Don't even let that thought linger, Hildy. I just saw him, and he's asking the same questions you are. They're all waiting in the living room for you, and I've never seen Jimmy so antsy to get things started. Just relax, Hon. It'll all be fine."

She leaned forward, offering a dainty hug, and was interrupted by a timid knock sounding on the closed bedroom door. Heather swished her skirts around to answer it, opening to her ancient friend, wrapped neatly in a black tuxedo, complete with bowtie.

"Well, I'll be..." Cyrus' eyes twinkled as he sized Hildy from head to toe. "Ain't you just the prettiest thing I've ever seen? Jimmy won't know what hit him." He chuckled to himself at his friend's imagined response. "Are you ready, then? I bet this is the first wedding ever where the best man is the fill-in father of the bride. I'm gonna have to do some fancy manoeuvring, huh?"

Hildy smiled, allowing Cyrus' light humour to ease her tension, and offered her trademark peck on the weathered, bristly cheek. Heather stood by, watching as Cyrus cleared his throat and allowed the middle-aged woman to fuss over his tie and boutonnière. And then it was time, and Heather, drawing a calming breath, began the small procession leading down the hall to the crowded living room, converted into a chapel for that very special day.

Cyrus and Hildy followed, the older man strutting like a proud papa with the bride on his arm, Hildy blushing with the freshness of every bride before her who had taken the walk that led to the joining of two souls.

The music, a CD of old romance songs, played softly in the background, setting the stage for the main event. Jimmy gaped openly at his bride, his heart leaping through his eyes at her. Smiles covered faces and tears filled eyes as Cyrus handed Hildy to her intended and repeated the phrase "I do" to the question of "Who gives this woman to be wed?" He then, amidst a smattering of chuckles, stepped as discreetly as possible to Jimmy's side, preparing for his next part.

Angus stood before them and led them through their vows, guiding them in the solemn pledge that is called marriage, counselling as he told them of their responsibilities to each other—and then it was finished. The rings were exchanged. The promises made. And they kissed, long and warmly, and turned to face the small group before them.

"It is my great joy and pleasure to introduce all of you to my friends and co-workers in the faith, Mr. and Mrs. James Billington!"

Applause burst the air, shattering the hovering silence as the clerics, the soon to be residents of Christ's Redeemed, a few friends, and Heather's family cheered and welcomed the new couple.

Again, Heather caught David's disconcerting glance, and her face coloured as she interpreted the emotion he allowed her to see. Lifting her chin, she returned his look, a playful challenge in her eyes. His own expression softened, a mischievous grin lifting one corner of his mouth, and then the newlyweds were past him, moving to the hallway and into the elevator.

They continued the celebration in the park where Jimmy and Hildy had first met so many years before, eating, and chatting together as a group. Those in the street community who knew the couple, even vaguely, edged closer to the celebration and were quickly drawn in to share in their happiness. Vagabonds and bridal party stood, interspersed, as photos were snapped and food was passed around. The couple made certain none of the street folk were overlooked in the busyness of the afternoon.

Dusk came and the party wound down, hobos returning to their benches or alleys and family and guests heading back to the shelter. For the first time in her life, Hildy felt shy as Jimmy escorted her into the taxi that would take them to their hotel.

He was worth millions and could have given her anything, but she refused the fancy car and extravagance that normally accompanied a wedding. She wanted their honeymoon to be like the life they had lived—simple and basic. Jimmy had agreed easily and she loved him the more for it.

Climbing into the cab amidst a hail of rice and confetti, they settled back into the far corner, snuggling in contentment as the car pulled from the curb, tin cans rattling a wedding herald from the back bumper. And they drove off into the night.

Ten

THE BATTER WAS SMOOTH AND SMELLED delicious as it oozed from the mixing bowl into the greased and floured cake pan, and Heather revelled in the feeling of accomplishment. Learning how to cook and clean had been an incredible challenge for both she and Hildy. Unlike Jimmy, who had left his organized life as an adult, the two women had spent too much of their learning years on the streets of Toronto.

She placed the pan into the heated oven and began the task of cleaning up her mess. It was hard to believe that it had been over two years since leaving the streets. Sometimes it was difficult. She missed the freedom and lack of responsibilities on occasion. Hildy struggled, too, Heather knew. But God was good, and He always answered their prayers for patience and endurance.

She threw a hurried glance at the clock and her heart skipped an excited beat. He was coming today. Glancing in the mirror above the sink, she shuddered. Flour lightly dusted one cheek and her hair fell in sweaty wisps across her forehead. She couldn't let him see her like this.

Heather looked one last time at the pan of goo beginning to heat in the oven, set the timer, and scrambled upstairs for a quick shower and change. She brushed past a freshly scrubbed Jimmy on the landing, and in so doing, caught her own reflection in the mirror that hung on the wall behind him. Heavens! She couldn't let her guest see her like this. Jimmy chuckled at the red-haired tornado as she flew by and shook his head while continuing down to the common room to await the arrival of their special Thanksgiving company.

Chapter Ten…

Showers of Blessing

THE THREE-AND-A-HALF-HOUR DRIVE to Christ's Redeemed halfway house ate a huge chunk out of the time they would normally use for building and working. They rotated in groups just so the work could continue non-stop. It was amazing how many churches willingly donated time and materials for the project, and the committee was thrilled with the generosity of the community in spite of their lack of financial need.

Heather, Charlie, and Cyrus often took the weekend shifts and the others went during the week, all of them supervising and monitoring the progress of the hired and volunteer work crews. In such a way, the log structure rose to its rustic grandeur quickly and was decorated and furnished sooner than anyone had thought possible.

Heather enjoyed the long road trips to the small town nestled among towering pines, oaks and maples. She savoured the time spent with her brother, hearing about his teen years and the things he had accomplished and what he was still pursuing. Cyrus never failed to entertain with a funny story from off of the streets, and the bond between the three grew strong.

The weekends were quiet, the machinery still, the work crews gone, and the three would inspect the grounds, making suggestions and doing the small jobs that were left unfinished. Charlie and Cyrus would work together laying electrical cable and installing outlets. It was amazing the difference a week could make, and they enjoyed pointing out the progress made by Angus and the others on the structure itself.

Sunday afternoon would come and all three were reluctant to return to the city, but they knew Jimmy, Hildy, and Angus were just as eager to take their shift during the weekdays.

More and more, Heather found herself wondering what David would think of the progress on the building. She appreciated his willingness to listen as she eagerly babbled on about the accomplishments made each week.

Sometimes he would wander in from patrol duty, two coffees in hand, and sit for ten or fifteen minutes, listening attentively, asking questions, content to be there as long as she wanted him there. Other times—in his spare time—he would return to the shelter to work the food line alongside her, pouring kindness and attention on the downcast of the city, and Heather marvelled at his compassion.

Yes, she was reluctant to go back to the city, but she enjoyed her friendship with David and somehow felt a little empty when he wasn't around to share her delight in the advances made on the project.

And then the day came when it was all finished. The machines and men were gone, the debris was cleaned up, and before a small crowd rested an eight bedroom log facility ready to be filled with the sounds of laughter and tears and the many other elements that made up communal life.

The audience consisted of the clerics, the committee, the volunteers, a number of members from the Restoule community, and the first residents of Christ's Redeemed Halfway House. They stood solemnly on the lawn between the building and the lake, waiting for the opening ceremony and ribbon-cutting. Angus and Jane stood arm in arm beside Heather and Charlie. Tear-filled eyes looked on as Jimmy and Hildy approached the ribbon barring the doorway. Scissors in hand, they waited for the nod from Reverend Anderson, chair of the building committee, and neatly snipped the barrier in two to the accompaniment of powerful applause. Then they moved inside to celebrate in the large kitchen and common room.

Once, during the day, Heather caught David eyeing the building with a wistfulness she didn't understand, and then he turned, smiled, and requested a guided tour, paying close attention as she walked him through the smaller outbuildings to be used by paying campers. Together they inspected each building, impressed with the cozy simplicity of them. She thoroughly enjoyed the man's undivided attention and felt a pang of regret when he finally led her to his car, and offered his goodbyes.

It was a long, drawn out affair, and Heather sensed her friend's reluctance to leave. If he didn't have a night shift to complete, she was certain he would have found a reason to stay longer, but the sun was setting and they both knew he had a long drive ahead. Pouring himself into his compact car, David took one last, lingering look at Heather and then pulled away, leaving her standing alone, the evening chill wrapping itself around her as the last of the season's crickets called out their lonely tune.

Heather had slept in the new residence before, but not as a permanent inhabitant, and she felt a little shiver run through her as she assisted in the final cleanup before bed. For now, she had her own bedroom that she would later share with a newcomer. How long had it been since she had been in a bed she could call her own? Seven years on the street and one year at the mission was a long time to live without a place to call home. She could have moved in with her parents, but the apartment was small and she wasn't sure they would be able to handle some of the interesting side effects of living on the streets.

She glanced slyly at Jimmy and Hildy. They beamed at each other with a pride that comes to new homeowners. This was their first real home together and they shared their own excitement over it. One by one, the new residents would settle in over the following week, each finding their own niche. It would take time for the business end of the facility to function smoothly, but it would come.

Heather, for once in her life, felt home.

*   *   *

In a prison facility across the province, parole papers were being processed for one Andrew Cully, charged with murder, ordered to serve ten years, but released early for good behaviour. No one at the mission knew.

*   *   *

Life settled into a series of organized events for Heather and the others. The opening of the halfway house had taken place midway through the autumn season, and for that they were all grateful. It allowed them time to prepare for their first snowmobile camp. An instructor had been hired to teach all the residents how to safely operate the bulky winter machines and, although the snow was sparse and sporadic, each of them worked hard to master the clutch, throttle, and braking combination of the heavy toys in anticipation of the harsh months ahead.

The six small cabins that dotted the hillside standing guard over the larger main residence needed to be prepared for customers who had already booked for the premier season. The battle to keep spiders and bugs from inhabiting each empty cottage was an ongoing one, leaving Heather to shudder regularly at any newly discovered guests.

Wood was stacked to feed the small barrel-shaped stoves that provided heat, and bedding was delivered and neatly stored in cedar chests beside the rough-hewn beds that gave each small dwelling its ancient and rustic look.

One persistent visitor habitually drove the three hours to visit, offering help where needed, and even Heather, in her naivety, couldn't help but notice that David seemed to look for excuses to visit, staying until the last possible minute, returning to the city only to fulfill his duties.

She began to fret, uncertain what to do, unable to restrain her own growing affection for the young man, yet afraid that she wasn't worthy of such a good person. It was Hildy who finally confronted her about her own hypocrisy, chastising Heather for her lack of faith. She would never forget that tongue-lashing.

* * *

Heather paced uneasily for an hour after the phone call from David, her heart hungry for his company, her head telling her to give herself a shake.

Hildy had been baking bread for most of the afternoon, the large ovens chuffed full of plump, yeasty mounds of dough. The woman thrived on the work of mixing ingredients and kneading, but that job was finished and she had just settled down on the love seat in the common room for a moment of undisturbed reading when Heather drifted in, a distracted look plastered across her face.

The older woman watched her as she drifted from room to room, repeating a circuit she had already traversed several times, and finally Hildy set aside her book and crossed her arms, waiting for Heather to return to the common room once more.

"What do you think you're doing, girl?"

The question caught Heather off guard, snapping her out of her introspection as she stopped to face Hildy, blinking stupidly.

"What do you mean?"

"Just what I asked." Her friend rose and came to block her path.

"I was just thinking." It was lame and Heather knew it.

"You have a lot of nerve, Missy." Again Heather blinked as Hildy warmed to her subject, her voice carrying a touch of acid.

"You gave me that whole song and dance about trusting God to show me what was right when we lived at the mission and I wasn't a believer. Was it all a lie?"

Heather felt her own temper rising at the challenge from her friend.

"Of course not. Why would you think that?"

"Because here you are, falling in love with a good Christian man and worried sick about the whole thing." Hildy's bluntness knocked the wind completely out of Heather's sails and she nodded miserably.

"Yes, I am. But I don't know what to do. I've been praying about it. Do you think it's wrong…is it really that obvious?" She looked around her, suddenly anxious of prying ears.

"Yes, it is obvious, and no, you haven't prayed," Heather's brow furrowed at the continuing confrontation, "'cause if you had prayed and truly asked God to take care of it, you wouldn't be pacing around here all worried about whether it's right or not. You'd be doing whatever it is you're supposed to be doing without a second thought 'cause you'd know that God's looking after it and doesn't really need your help."

The girl dropped her head in shame, aware that her own words of faith had been neatly repackaged and tossed back at her. She drew in a breath and sighed, looking at the front door that sat closed in anticipation of its next guest.

"You're right, Hildy." An answering harrumph was all she got.

"So will you pray with me now?"

Hildy uncrossed her arms and took one of Heather's cool hands, leading her back to the love seat where they sat and bowed their heads.

"Jesus, here we are, at your feet again. Heather needs your help. You already know this but she's head over heels for David and doesn't think she's good enough for him..." At her friend's startled gasp, she opened one eye and redirected her words, "Yes, I do know that's what you're thinking, girl." Closing her eye again, she continued.

"As I was saying, Jesus, she thinks she's not good enough and is too daft to see that David is just as crazy over her. Lord, we're asking for two things here. Help both of these love-struck kids know your will about this relationship...and help them not to waste time with it like Jimmy and I did. In Jesus' name...oh and for goodness sake, make Heather relax a bit. Her pacing is driving me nuts. Amen."

Heather sat back, amused by the directness of the brief prayer, and thanked her friend, feeling a peace about the upcoming visit. She watched as Hildy returned to her book, burying herself in its pages and felt, again, incredible gratitude for such a true and honest friend.

She didn't know how long she had dozed but was startled awake awhile later by the ringing of the doorbell. Her cheek bore the wrinkles of the throw cushion she had rested her face on and her hair had a slightly mussed look about it. Panic seized her as Hildy opened the door, admitting David, still in his uniform and looking pristine. It was too late to do anything about her appearance, so she simply endured the mischief dancing in his eyes as he came to stand before her, his gaze drinking in every part of her appearance, lined cheek, messy hair and all.

"Hey."

"Hey, yourself," was her only reply as Heather worked her fingers through the short red waves, trying to tame them while he watched, amused by her efforts. They stood, awkwardly avoiding eye contact, not knowing what to say for what seemed an eternity until the silence was broken by Hildy's exasperated sigh.

Setting her book aside once more, the tactless woman approached, placed an arm around each shoulder and turned the young couple toward the front door, herding them like sheep.

"Why don't you two love birds go for a walk or something? Maybe you'll find something out there that will help you get over this shy nonsense and get on with what's really on both of your minds."

Heather and David drew back in unison, shocked and embarrassed to the core by the older woman's boldness. Neither knew whether to be angry with her or to laugh, but Hildy continued, fully aware of their discomfort but not put off by it.

"Look, you two…I don't mean to be insensitive, but life is too short to be pussy-footin' around any topic, especially one this important. Now, I love you both and I've broken the ice for you. You can hate me later, but for now, there's no excuse for you both to ignore what the rest of us can see so clearly. We all know you like each other. Now you need to find out if you're right for each other. So go on. Get out into the beautiful garden God made and talk."

With that, she dropped her arms, turned, and walked back to her comfortable perch, picking her book up and once again burying herself in its pages. Heather looked shyly up at her companion, relieved by the amused expression on David's face, and turned to the wall hooks for her wool coat.

Once outside, they relaxed, enjoying the crispness of the late afternoon air. A light dusting of snow had covered the remnants of the previous small storm and the ground crunched beneath their feet.

"So, how was the drive here?" Heather's breath frosted the air, drifting like wafts of smoke. David stopped her, turning her gently with one hand until she faced him.

"You know, Heather, Hildy's right. As much as I'm not really keen on her matchmaking methods, she has me pegged pretty thoroughly. I am head over heels for you and have been for quite some time. I don't have a ring, but I've thought a lot about buying one. I just wasn't sure you'd accept it."

Although his voice was strong, it carried a slight waver as he laid his heart on the line, and Heather didn't know whether to laugh with joy or cry with despair. She turned her face away, staring off toward the island as it slept peacefully in the lake's embrace. Trying to gather her thoughts carefully, she focused her attention on the island's main inhabitant, a large and industrious beaver, who at that moment was trying hard to manoeuvre a large birch branch down the shore to the water's edge.

"David, I've grown very fond of you, too. And yes, Hildy is right that I should be upfront with you. I lived a pretty awful life for several years. I enjoyed some of it, but most of it I'd rather forget. Unfortunately, I can't. I've done things that I'm ashamed of and there are parts of me that I've given away…that I can't get back. It's not fair for you to have to live with a woman who isn't complete—who isn't pure. I can't be selfish that way."

With his finger, David drew her face back to his. Gently, he traced the length of the puckered scar that ran down the contours of her cheek. His gaze was warm but determined, and a part of her cried with an anguish that comes from being so close to what you want but at the same time fearing you'll never be able to attain it.

"Is this what you're talking about?" he continued to caress the reminder of her harsh past. "Because if it is, you need to know a few things about me too. I know about Andy. It hasn't been a real big secret. You have no idea how much I prayed for you when I heard you'd become his plaything. You see, I've been drawn to you since that first day I saw you standing in the soup line, ragged, cold and hungry.

Don't think I didn't have quite a struggle with that. I knew you were only about fourteen, and there I was, twenty-three, a rookie cop and a new Christian." He smiled at her surprise and continued.

"Oh yes…I'd only been saved for about three months, but it was long enough for me to know that I couldn't have you. So I started praying for you. I didn't know about the demon, but I was pretty sure you were a runaway, and when you disappeared and I heard what Cyrus had done, I was furious."

A lone tear squeezed past Heather's lowered lashes, tracking its way down her cheek, dipping into the scar's groove to finish its path to her chin before David wiped it away with a tender thumb.

"As for not being complete…well I don't believe that for a moment. Last time I checked, Jesus' dying words were 'It is finished.' I would say that's pretty complete, wouldn't you? You did put your trust in him, didn't you?"

Heather kept her gaze lowered, but nodded her head with emphasis.

"You asked for his forgiveness?"

Again the nod.

"So it is finished—completed—making you a completed woman in Christ. Ok?"

One more nod finished her unspoken part of the conversation.

"As I said earlier, you don't know about my past, either. I grew up in a God-fearing family in the city, but that's no guarantee that a kid will take the right path. I got into some stupid things. Fortunately, I didn't get caught.

"When I hit high school and a cop came to do a presentation, I knew I wanted that kind of authority so I smartened up and did all the stuff I needed to do in order to become one. I got pretty full of myself when I got accepted to Police College at such a young age. I got good grades and took the job I've got now when I had a chance. All that power can go to a man's head and it did. I got cocky and bossy with some of the street punks, throwing my weight around like I was God.

"One night, I was on patrol, messing with a hooker just for the fun of it…nothing serious…just mouthing off to her. Her pimp saw me and figured I was harassing her, trying to get one more notch on my belt by busting her."

This time, David pulled his eyes away to watch the island's hardworking rodent as it waddled into the water with its cumbersome prize. Heather was certain that he didn't really see the beaver as she studied the clenched jaw and withdrawn expression.

"He started giving me a rough time, telling me I was hassling his girlfriend and he'd call his lawyer if I didn't back off. I was mouthy then, thinking I knew it all, and I told him I'd haul his sorry backside into the pen for trafficking in prostitution if he didn't shut-up. That's when things got messy. His girl took off when he drew his knife.

"For the first time in my life, I didn't know what to do and all my bravado was gone. He must have seen the fear in my eyes, because he made his move. I don't remember drawing my gun, but I must have, because the next thing I knew, he was lying on the ground with a bullet hole in his chest. He died almost instantly, and it was all because I had an ego problem."

David drew in a wavering breath, releasing it harshly and as he forced himself to continue.

"They gave me a pat on the back for it. Heather, I provoked a man and then shot him. They tried to convince me that it was self-defence, and I guess it was in a way, but I can't help thinking that if I hadn't been such an arrogant jerk he would still be alive today. I've often wondered if I'd be capable of drawing a gun on a man again. I've been fortunate so far not to have had to find out.

"Anyway, that was the beginning of my journey toward seeking God. He's taught me a lot about forgiveness and love…and…" He turned back to Heather, drinking in her beauty with his cobalt stare, "…patience."

Taking her small hand in his larger one, David smiled down at her, thrilling in the true feelings that swam in her wide eyes.

"All this time, I was worried that the nine year difference was what bothered you. Do you care?" Heather's eyes never left his as her soft answer rang through the silence.

"No."

"You see, Heather. We both have our ghosts from the past and God has overcome them. Do you think we could give it a try? I love you and want you to be my wife, but I want you to be sure. Can you be?"

Heather smiled then, her own love bursting from her, and she stepped closer, allowing him—begging him—to draw her into a firm embrace. His mouth lowered, drawn to hers with a magnetism that defied all resistance, and they kissed. All that they had ever heard or read about love's first kiss, all that could ever be imagined, became reality and they knew that it was the beginning of something pure and beautiful.

Eleven

THE SWEET AND ADDICTING FRAGRANCE of carrot cake wafted through the air, drawing more and more attention to the kitchen. Heather towel-dried her hair quickly, knowing that if she could smell her cake upstairs, it must be pretty close to being done.

She glanced quickly at her bedside alarm clock and quickened her pace. There were advantages to shorter hair, she mused, as she dragged a comb through the damp curls. She was certainly glad she had thought of mixing up the cream cheese icing beforehand, and hoped no one had decided to sample it. "Sampling" in the halfway house usually meant you had to make a batch all over again.

Never a person for makeup, Heather checked her appearance one last time, put on some chapstick and headed for the stairs, fretting as the smell of cake grew stronger. Just in time, the frazzled woman entered the kitchen, spying Jimmy, icing bowl in one hand and spoon in the other, heading for a chair, and she quickly rescued her concoction.

"That's for the cake, which, if my nose is correct, is done. If you eat the icing now, you don't get any cake later. And I'm not leaving this kitchen before you."

She patted him lovingly on the head as he sat there, empty-handed with a mock pout on his face. The mournful expression didn't last long as he turned in his chair and watched his young friend remove the large confection from the oven and place it in the refrigeration unit to cool quickly. The bowl of icing went next to it and a quickly penned note was placed on top of the plastic wrap that once again covered the bowl. It read a simple warning and Jimmy chuckled at the threat.

"Do you honestly think that threatening someone with bodily harm is going to keep them from one of your amazing cakes? That young David is going to get fat quick once you two are married." Jimmy chuckled to himself, shaking his head as a thought occurred to him.

"I still can't believe he was able to get a job with the OPP in Powassan. What a blessing to have him so close, eh?"

He watched her reaction and smiled gently when Heather glanced down at the diamond ring glittering merrily on the third finger of her left hand. Absently, she rolled it back and forth with her thumb.

"Have you two picked a date yet?"

Heather turned, light dancing in her eyes as she was overcome with excitement.

"It isn't final, and I should be telling my family and Hildy this first since you tried to steal my icing, but we're thinking May fourteenth of this coming spring. That gives us half a year to get ready, which, I might add, was a whole lot more time than you and Hildy gave us." She wrinkled her nose mischievously at him and turned back to the sink to wash the lettuce for the salad.

"We're a lot older. We didn't have the time to waste."

Heather stopped, turning to assess the deadpan expression, and then burst out laughing, Jimmy joining her as she continued her kitchen duties.

Chapter Eleven...

Ghost From the Past

WHY SHE HAD AGREED TO GO BACK to the mission with Cyrus and Charlie in this kind of weather, she didn't know. Heather squeezed her eyes into a strained squint, trying to distinguish between the passenger side of the road and the ditch through the fat white flakes of snow that swirled hypnotically through the air. Cyrus sat in the back seat, silent but frightened. Heather didn't need to look back to know that he was praying again. She could hear his muttering clearly and could imagine him, head bowed, hands clasped firmly before him as he approached God with petitions of mercy. She glanced to her left and studied Charlie, hunched over the steering wheel, blue eyes searching ahead for the sign that he had longed to see an hour earlier. A wisp of dark hair spilled over his forehead and some instinct prominent in older sisters made her ache to brush it back so he could see better.

"There it is!"

She looked through the windshield past the slapping wipers to glimpse the outline of the half-buried sign that marked the entrance to the city of Toronto. She breathed a small sigh of relief, knowing they didn't have far to go. They were already running two hours late and she knew her parents would be frantic with worry. Why would anyone in their right mind venture out with a snowstorm brewing? She tried to relax back against the battered upholstery of the ancient vehicle as they cruised into the heart of the city amidst increasing winds, and shuddered at the unoccupied carcasses of vehicles that hadn't been so lucky to reach their destinations.

*   *   *

It was dark by the time the three pulled the weary car into the mission's snow-filled parking lot. After much manoeuvring, they managed to bury the heavy old dinosaur in a drift of snow and resigned themselves to having to leave it there until a tow truck could come. Unloading their parcels and luggage, the tired travelers waded awkwardly to the entrance, relieved that they would soon be inside, safe and warm.

"I can't believe you three drove all the way from Restoule in this storm." Although Jane spoke in a level voice, Heather recognized the anxious undertones and quickly hugged her mother reassuringly.

"Well, we made it and I'd better call Hildy or she'll be having fits."

True to Heather's prediction, Hildy had much to say about the foolishness of the young, but Heather knew the woman was venting out her worry and was glad they had made it safely. Dropping their bundles onto the floor by the entrance, they huddled around the radiator with steaming cups of apple cider warming their hands.

Heather looked around the common room, which was packed to the rafters with people driven to seek shelter in the freezing blizzard. The sight of so many displaced people, lost and without hope, never failed to move her deeply.

Meanwhile, one small bundled figure had escaped notice, and Shorty hunkered down deeper in her odd assortment of winter wear. She had seen the arrival of the three wanderers and immediately recognized them. Her eyes narrowed with bitterness as she observed them covertly.

"It was all that Heather's fault," she muttered to herself, and pulled the half-frozen dog closer to her chest, burying it within the ratty rags of her thin coat. If she hadn't come to the park, Hildy would still be with her, protecting her and finding her food. The brat had ruined it all. Forgotten was the fact that Hildy, Jimmy, Cyrus, and Heather had all pleaded with her on numerous occasions to join them up in the hinterlands of Northern Ontario. The archaic and faulty memory failed to prod her to recall her own responses of bitter and angry rejection. The only theme that repeated itself over and over in her addled mind was that Heather was responsible for the difficult conditions the old woman had found herself in.

Quickly she finished her soup and discreetly worked her way through the crowd, slipping through the door out into the winter blast. Huddling against the bitter wind that tore through her shabby coverings, turning her lips blue and causing shivers to course through her wrinkled body, she cradled her poor shivering canine closer to share its heat. She looked back often, making sure no one followed as she worked her way along a familiar street and ducked into a side door left unlocked for a purpose such as this.

"What do you want, you old hag?"

The man was bored and had no intention of being hassled for food by some filthy bum. He hated guard duty but didn't mind collecting the money that came with the job. He also hated his boss's penchant for attracting the scum of the city to keep him informed of its underworld's intricate workings. He'd just as soon see the side door locked and let the bums freeze.

"I'm here to see Andy."

Her teeth chattered and her voice was dry and crackly.

"Is that so? And who do you think you are?" The man stood and swaggered toward her, causing her to cower against the wall.

"I have news for him. It's about Heather." She blurted the name out in fear and the guard stopped, ready to listen.

"What about her?"

Shorty was no fool. She'd hustled on the streets for far too long to hand information over so easily.

"I'm not telling you anything. If Andy wants to know about Heather, it's going to be me telling him."

She had edged her way to the door, ready for a quick exit if the occasion arose, but the guard decided it wasn't worth the effort and radioed his boss.

"Yah, Andy, I got a little old lady here who says she's got something to tell you about Heather…yah…ok." He put the radio aside and pointed to a door at the end of a long hallway. Lifting his nose in the air and adopting a stuffy British accent, he imperiously informed her, "Mr. Cully will see you now." He chuckled at his own little joke and Shorty rolled her eyes as she shuffled her bulk toward the indicated room.

She was wary as she timidly knocked on the heavy oak door. A muffled voice clipped off a quick command to enter and she wasted no time. Shocked by the change that had taken place in Andy, Shorty hesitated in the doorway. He no longer had that slick con-man look about him. Prison had hardened him—and deadened him. He had muscled out, no doubt about that, and he no longer wore fancy clothing. Jeans and a sweatshirt replaced the suit and bold tie that he was known to wear. His head was bald and a skull tattoo covered it. She shuddered as she looked into eyes that had been to hell and back, instantly regretting her decision to come pay him a visit.

"What can I do for you? Damon says you have information on Heather." He frowned in concentration as he eyed the old woman from head to shivering toe.

"I remember you. Yes, you were one of Heather's…ah…companions in the park."

Shorty nodded, suddenly at a loss for words, and she swallowed hard.

Andy sat back in his chair and watched the old bat through hooded eyes. She was scared. That was good. He enjoyed the fear. It made him feel powerful. But Andy was smart. Treat the hag with respect and honour and he could get what he'd been dreaming about for years—Heather.

He didn't like to admit it, but she owned his soul; or rather, the beast inside of her did. Many times he had to shake himself free of the obsessive dreams he had. He hungered for her, craved her. He wanted her badly. And he would truly enjoy disciplining her for her little act of rebellion.

He counted it to Heather's credit that he had lost his cool with one of his new strippers, beating her to death. She'd had the nerve to look too much like the woman of his dreams, and he hated being reminded that she had left him. He couldn't believe how badly it had affected him to see her near carbon copy. One of his boys had hired her, thinking it would ease the foul mood that had lingered for months after his girl had run. What the surveillance cameras didn't show the cops was how he had carved up his man to remind him never to do something so stupid again.

He smiled and Shorty cringed. The smile was merely a thin line stretched across a mask of evil, and she began to shake. He sat there, wicked grin hovering, and watched her squirm like a fish caught in a net. And then he pulled out some money and brought it to her, pressing it gently into her hand.

"You need some better clothes, madam. And by the looks of it, some decent food. This ought to help. Now, what can you tell me about Heather?"

He smiled again, this time relaxing the clenched jaw muscles enough to give him a pleasant cast—almost. Shorty stared at the money in awe. She had never seen so much cash before. Lifting her gaze from the bills to her benefactor, she began to talk, spilling the words out in a rush of reluctant willingness.

"Your Heather is back at the mission. She arrived a half hour ago with her brother and that old coot, Cyrus. I heard the rumour on the streets that you wanted information about them just last week or I'd been in sooner."

"I only got out last week…so tell me, what you did find,…what's your name?"

"Call me Shorty…and this here dog is Whip. Yah…I'd forgotten that you've been in the pen. So you've missed a lot. Heather got religion. So did Cyrus, Hildy and one-eyed Jimmy. They been working at the mission for the past year or so. She's got a ring on her finger and Hildy and Jimmy are married. I'm no fool. I steered clear of all that hokey stuff. Anyways, Heather got dragged in there by the gang and them reverend guys did some talking and fancy stuff and she let out a God-awful screech and the fits stopped. She ain't had one since." She stopped, worried like a cowed animal, wondering if she had made a bad choice by coming to Andy.

He waved his hand impatiently, trying to sift through the flood of information, grasping the more important details to savour.

"Hold on, my lady. What is this about a ring? You don't mean Heather, do you?"

Shorty swallowed hard, knowing she had struck a nerve and was uncertain how to safely continue. She watched, feeling trapped like a bird before a hungry cat, and her mouth worked nervously.

"The cop that works there...David somebody or other...he...she...they are getting married. Least that's what I've been told. I never saw the ring but it was Whiskey what told me, and his buddy is a police informant, so I guess it must be true."

His eyes narrowed angrily, but Andy kept his voice calm.

"Go on," he prodded.

"Well, the bunch of them started working at the mission and they come up with some fancy place up in the woods where people could go to get off the streets and start over again. She's been living there for quite some time but she just come back to the mission for the weekend. I imagine she'll be spending time with her police friend so I don't know how easy it would be for you to get to her. That's all I know."

The old woman clamped her mouth firmly closed and looked once more at the money, clutching it close to her chest with one hand while holding the mutt still on her lap. Andy scanned her from head to toe, committing her looks to memory in case he needed her again, and then nodded for her to be dismissed.

*   *   *

Shorty caught the gesture and grasped at it like one grasping at a reprieve from a death sentence. She licked her cracked lips and rose from the chair. Looking one last time at the cash, the old hobo turned and bolted from the room, not stopping to even look at the guard as she made her way to the safety of the street.

*   *   *

Andy sat still, allowing his mind to process all he had learned. So she got religion huh? And she'd replaced him. He mentally shrugged. That didn't matter. It wouldn't take long. He had learned a lot in prison. He knew what had lived inside of Heather, and given the right circumstances, he was sure he could return her to her previous state. Oh yes. He had learned much.

*   *   *

Shorty leaned against the cold brick wall in the alley three streets over from Andy's building. Her heart pounded with fear as her eyes shifted furtively from side to side. So quick was her exit that she had only had time to stuff the cash in her shabby coat pockets, but she was crafty enough to know that it wouldn't be safe there long.

She adjusted her weight, trying to relieve the pain in her half frozen feet as she worked her way deeper into the secluded alley. She knew where the storm drain was but she wasn't sure whether she'd be able to pry it open in the freezing weather. She shuffled along quickly, her shrewd gaze dodging around her, searching for the place, all the while trying to keep watch against intruders.

Turning a corner, she heaved a sigh of relief at what was before her. There in the center of the alley, steam pouring through its slotted surface, was a great iron disk lying level with the pavement. Shorty threw one last glance over a shivering shoulder and squatted, working stiff fingers into the cold, damp cracks.

She was in luck as she felt the heavy metal cover shift, and with much effort she slid it to the side and shimmied her way through the opening, pulling it back in place above her as she lowered herself onto the ladder below.

It stank. Pure, foul, stench. But it was dry at the bottom of the ladder and that's all she needed. Below the small platform that supported the ladder, a dark river of sludge oozed by, the rotting sewage providing enough heat to keep her fingers from freezing as she greedily counted the bills. Two hundred dollars. A veritable fortune to an old woman who had nothing.

Her conscience tweaked with its distant, gentle voice and she allowed herself to question the act that had brought her the cash. She had betrayed Heather. But hadn't the girl betrayed her? A vision of the young lady floated before her mind's eye, smiling gently at her, offering her some small scrap of food. Arms that should have worked to keep themselves warm, wrapped around old shoulders in comfort.

Shorty shook her head angrily, forcing the image to dissipate. Heather was nice back then. But then she ruined it all with that religious stuff. The woman looked at the money again and smiled. In her twisted mind she rationalized it, telling herself that Heather would have wanted her to have the money. The girl could take care of herself. After all, hadn't she been able to stay away from Andy for this long?

What would she do with the money? She stuffed it into an inner pocket in the shabby coat and pulled herself back up the rusted ladder. It was harder to move the cap but she managed, grunting with the effort. Once out in the cold winter air, she shivered again and slinked her way to the alley's exit, planning her shopping spree as she went.

* * *

A scream tore from Heather's throat as she bolted upright in bed and sweat poured down her face, drenching her nightgown. Her mother rushed into her room, worry etched on the beautiful dark brow. Jane sat on the bed and put her arms around her shivering daughter, rocking her gently until she calmed enough to talk.

"It was awful, Mom." She drew in a ragged breath and released it as her mother loosened the comforting embrace.

"Tell me about it." Jane stroked Heather's forehead as though she were a young child, calming her with her gentle touch. Heather suffered another violent shudder, recalling the vivid nightmare that had shattered her sleep, and she buried her face against the long silky curtain that was her mother's slowly greying hair.

"It was Andy. I saw him in my dream. He had a black cape on and he was calling out to me. Beside him stood a monster like you can't imagine. It was huge and scaly and it had the word 'anger' stamped on its forehead like a name. Its claws were immense and it was drooling over a piece of paper with my name written on it. The name was written in blood—Andy's blood. When I looked at it, it smiled and beckoned me to come to it. It was hideous, Mom, but a part of me wanted to go. And then I heard a strong voice call out, 'No, she is mine—you can no longer have her,' and the monster disappeared."

She shivered as the dream washed over her again.

Jane wasted no time and placed her hand on Heather's head. The prayer burst forth with strength and victorious power, and

Heather felt the reassurance and confidence of one bought by the redeeming blood of Jesus. Immediately, she remembered the firm voice of her dream and knew it was the voice of her Saviour, claiming her, acknowledging her new birth and her position of adoption into his family of saints.

"Great Father, we draw close to you for your protection. The enemy has come against Heather again and we need your strength and power. We are weak, unable to conquer the evil one and his minions, but you, Lord—you have overcome the world. We turn this moment of battle over to you and trust you to protect us from the enemy's snare. In Jesus' all-powerful name. Amen."

Heather reached up and hugged her mother in gratitude, rolled over and drifted off to sleep. Jane watched her for some time, thanking God repeatedly for her deliverance and salvation and praying silently over her, and then she rose quietly and padded off to her own warm bed.

* * *

Andy stormed through the apartment's darkened basement in fury. She was so close. He could almost see her and then something had blocked him. His hand throbbed where he had drawn a knife across his palm, gathering the blood into an inkwell to write Heather's name on the parchment before the altar. He had felt the power and strength of his spirit guide and knew that it was merely a matter of time before he had enough power to consume her. He must have done something wrong, because his guide had been there with him, calling out to Heather, willing them to join their spirits with his—and then he was gone. Vanished. And Andy felt hollow and disoriented until his own wrath kicked in. It was a good thing he had kidnapped that hooker's brat to sacrifice. The spirit could have just as easily turned against him without the blood of an innocent human. As it was, killing the baby had likely covered whatever mistake Andy had made in his incantations.

He began jogging up the fifteen flights of stairs to his apartment, burning up the adrenalin that surged through his veins from his spiritual encounter. Heather was still as beautiful, but her hair was short. That would change, he told himself, as he recalled the visions of the long strands of silky fire.

He had revelled in the exhilaration that came with seeing her sleeping. His spirit guide had done it for him. He could feel his blood beginning to pound with desire, so he shifted his train of thought in another direction. His mind drifted to his years in prison as he continued the demanding trek upward.

He had always been fascinated with power, and when the opportunity arose for him to join a secret club within the prison, Andy had jumped at the chance. The members taught him much about gaining strength through contact with the dead. It had drawn him, and he had become obsessed with learning as much as he could. It wasn't long before he was requesting books that showed him how to conjure up spirits and use them to get what he wanted.

He soon took charge of the club, with a little help from his otherworld friends. In the short time he spent behind bars, Andy delved deeply into the cultic arts, gaining strength in his chosen vocation and teaching the other inmates to fear and respect him.

Finally reaching his destination, he entered his apartment and poured himself a drink, promising to tend to his wound later. Now that he had Heather's name written in his blood, he wouldn't have to cut himself again for a while. The rest of the blood had been smeared on the baby, mixing with its blood to endow him with even more power.

The run up the stairs had done a good job in calming Andy and he tossed the remainder of his drink back and returned to the basement to tidy up the ceremonial room. He probably should learn to control his temper a little better, but to be so close to Heather and not succeed was unbearable.

He looked at the altar, noting the absence of the sacrifice, and nodded. Damon must have disposed of the body. He never asked where his number one man dumped them, but none ever showed up, so what did he care? He blew out all but one candle and carried it to a small corner of the room where a large ancient-looking book rested. Opening the evil tome, Andy immersed himself, hoping to find what he had missed in his effort to consume Heather.

* * *

Damon was a practical man—a complete compliment to his flamboyant and high-strung boss and friend. He didn't understand any of this voodoo stuff or whatever it was, and he couldn't really care less. Andy was smart. And he was good to Damon. That was all that mattered. To a young man who had a prison record and no family, it was the best that could be hoped for.

The bundle he carried, tucked carefully under his arm, was light and small. No one paid any attention to the foot-long box wrapped neatly in bright and colourful Christmas wrapping paper. It was the season, after all, thank goodness. Had anyone bothered to inquire, he would have shrugged and told them it was a gift for his friend. But no one cared.

He walked briskly in the crisp air of the winter night, nodding benignly to the few who passed him on the street. No one ever messed with Damon. You were always polite to a man who was six-foot-seven and weighed three hundred pounds.

He ducked into an alley, following it until it widened out into a nearly empty parking lot. From there, he hurried, crossing the lot to the rear entrance of the small crematorium where he knocked twice on a solid steel door.

A small, weaselly man with shifting, beady eyes cracked the door open a fraction, and upon seeing who it was, widened the space, allowing Damon to enter quickly. He wore a coverall with the crematorium's logo emblazoned tastefully on his breast pocket. Harry was a janitor.

His rat-like eyes flitted from the box on the table to the wad of bills in the giant's huge hands. He could almost taste the money and didn't care what was in the package as long as he was paid well.

No one would notice the small parcel tucked safely under the corpse that was ready to be cremated. No evidence. Andy would be pleased, Damon thought to himself as he flipped the thousand-dollar bundle over to the distasteful little man. He knew that Harry would someday meet the same fate as the small, mutilated child bundled into the box wrapped for a Christmas it would never see.

* * *

The old woman strolled down the crowded street, pleased with herself and her wily ways. With her small fortune she had purchased two thick sweaters, a pair of heavy jeans, and a pair of boots. Of course, she had gone to a second-hand store. People were so wasteful, dropping off nearly new clothing just so they could buy more—not that she cared what others did with their money.

Shorty kept her ratty winter coat. It covered the sweaters, keeping other vagrants from questioning her good fortune. It felt so good to wear clean, thick socks. Her feet were warm for the first time in weeks, causing her to smile at Andy's generosity. Telling him about Heather was a small cost for all she had received in return.

She ducked into a nearby café and parked herself at a corner booth, giving her a complete view of the room and the street. A tired, middle-aged woman sauntered up to her table, menu and order pad in hand, and raised her brows skeptically at the dirty old woman.

"I assume you have money to pay for your order?"

It was rude, and Shorty was instantly angry. Snatching out a bill from a dark nook in her jacket, she flipped it toward the woman and grabbed the offered menu.

"Yes, I can pay. Are you this rude to all your customers? Why don't you go do something constructive—like work? And send someone to my table who has a few more manners."

The woman harrumphed and flounced her way back to the kitchen. A few moments later, a younger girl came over and smiled pleasantly.

"Sorry about Corra. She's at the end of her shift and it makes her grouchy when she thinks she's going to be held later. Can I take your order, ma'am?"

Shorty sniffed disdainfully and then, with much pomp and ceremony, ordered a massive breakfast of bacon, eggs, waffles, and toast. She gorged herself, smacking and chomping noisily in her hurry to satisfy her hunger. When she was finished, she rose, paid her bill and left, moving down the street slowly.

Food tends to make one complacent. It dulls the senses and causes a person to become drowsy and inattentive. So it was that Shorty never saw the car pull up carefully alongside her. Nor was she particularly aware that the door had opened. It wasn't until a large hand clamped onto her arm, pulling her hurriedly inside, that she realized she was in trouble.

Damon said nothing as he easily settled the little old lady beside him. It had been an effortless job since she was so small, but he was surprised at her lack of fight. He glanced sideways at her and cringed as he watched her chew a filthy fingernail. She felt his stare and threw a nervous look his way.

"I'm not worried none, young man. I know this here is Andy's car and he was real good to me the last time we talked."

He smiled and focused his stare out the window as the car pulled away from the curb. This was his city. He loved it—as much as a killer and bully could love. He thought about the earlier conversation he had with Andy and thought to himself, "If this bat knew what Andy has in mind, she'd be terrified." He said nothing and continued to enjoy the view from the tinted glass of the limousine.

* * *

Andy glided slowly around the chair that held the older woman. He guessed her to be around sixty years old, but who knew with street trash. They all looked ancient. She was nervous. That was good. He didn't want her to have a heart attack, though, so he kept his craving for blood in check.

"Well…uh…Shorty. So I've been around the mission a fair bit and can't seem to find a way to get to Heather. It appears you were right, my friend."

He stopped the circling and settled his backside against the edge of his desk, crossing his arms and watching her, delighting in her uncomfortable squirming.

"What do you think we should do about it, my dear?"

The old woman shrugged, adopting a careless attitude, and began picking the dirt from her cuticles in an attempt to distance herself from what she had set in motion.

"I don't know what you should do about it, but my job's done. You didn't pay me to do anything."

Andy struck quickly, like an adder, grasping the old woman's neck in a sturdy grip and squeezing only lightly. Her eyes bugged at the swift attack and he could feel her pulse accelerating through the flabby skin of her throat. It would be so easy to squeeze the life from the piece of garbage, but then he still wouldn't have what he wanted.

With reluctance, he released her and stepped back, eyeing her through narrowed lids. She trembled visibly as her mouth worked hard, trying to draw in air. He waited until her gasping had slowed and the submissive attitude had returned to the wide, watery eyes.

"Don't, for a second, think that I only purchased information, Shorty. I purchased you. I paid for you and whatever you can give me. As long as you continue to be of use, I will continue to pay you. When you are of no use, I will dispose of you. Don't ever cross me again. Do you understand?"

She nodded, terrified by the controlled and quiet tone in his voice as he spoke his threats to her.

"I want you to go back to the mission, old girl. I want you to find some way to get Heather to come outside alone. Get her to the back alley and we'll take it from there. I'll pay you well for that. As long as you do as you're told, it will be well worth your while. Damon and I are going for a coffee. You have a few minutes to think it over. When we come back, I'll be expecting your answer."

She nodded, relief flooding her as the two evil men left the room, closing the door behind them.

"What do you think?"

"I think she's weak and useless. It would be easy for her to turn on us once you have Heather."

"What do you suggest?"

Damon smiled his greedy, frightening smile.

"You let me and Willy look after it. We'll get you Heather and deal with the old girl."

* * *

She searched the room frantically, looking for something that would help her draw Heather out of the shelter. She knew she was dead if she didn't have some sort of plan in mind by the time the two thugs returned. A thought of pure hate wormed its way into her mind. It was Heather's fault again. She deserved it. Shorty was resigned to it. She would hand over the girl and everything would go back to the way it was.

The desk lay before her, tidy and sterile-looking. A beer stein held an assortment of pens and pencils at the top corner and just below it lay a note pad with "The Cully Club" embossed on the bottom in small tasteful print. An idea fingered its way into her fear-laced thoughts and she smiled a little, feeling a burst of adrenaline as she reached for the paper.

With a slow flick of her arthritic wrist, Shorty pulled a clean sheet from the pad and turned it over. With a pen, she began scrawling her brief message on the paper, putting as much sincerity into it as she could. When it was finished, she returned everything to its place and sat back in her chair, reading the message over and over, relaxing more with each passing moment.

Andy was surprised at how calm the old girl was when he and Damon slipped back into his office. He figured she'd either be dead on the floor from heart failure, or she would have tried to escape, allowing them to follow her discreetly, hoping she would draw Heather out just from fear.

He didn't expect her to be sitting, relaxed, in the same chair, a crumpled piece of paper hanging from her dirt-encrusted fingers. She drew her lips back in a rotted-tooth smile and handed him the smudged and wrinkled sheet. Impressive, he thought to himself. Simple enough that it wouldn't raise suspicion, but effective. Andy nodded and handed the scrap back to her.

"Very good, Shorty. You are quite an industrious lady. Damon…" he turned to his friend. "Could you escort our companion back to the mission, please? And make sure you take a treat down to her little pet. I'm sure he wasn't very happy being left in the car without her."

Damon nodded and helped the tramp to her feet, patiently guiding her from the office, throwing one last glance Andy's way. The two exchanged a look, both men hungering for violence. And then Damon closed the door behind himself.

* * *

"But Jesus can love you, Jenny. He died for you and wants you to be free from the stuff you're doing now."

Heather's voice was filled with compassion as she pleaded with the sixteen-year-old prostitute. The girl and two of her associates sat huddled at a table in the common room, listening to the words of hope that the ex-street girl offered. All three knew Heather and had, on occasion, witnessed some of her fits. All three knew she no longer had those fits and wanted to know why. That was forty minutes ago, but the more they talked the more confused they became.

"So you're saying that Jesus can love me even though I'm a whore, but He wants me to stop being a whore. That's impossible, Heather. If Danny even knew we were here, he'd beat the crap out of us. I can't imagine what he'd do if I told him I wasn't hooking anymore."

Heather sympathized. So many of these girls had come to the city with dreams of becoming something great, only to have those dreams dashed by the deception of street prostitution. Once a pimp got hold of a girl it was very difficult for her to get free. Heather understood and they knew she understood.

"Let me show you something, Jenny. This is a Bible…"

"Yah, I know what a Bible is. I used to go to Sunday school until I was ten."

"Ok, so you know that it is a book that God had different people write to give us instructions on how to live. It's also a collection of historical events that can be backed up with archaeology and other history books. I want to read you a story that might help you to understand what Jesus thinks about prostitutes."

The three girls settled into their chairs as Heather flipped through the pages of the book set before her, finally settling on John 4:7-26. She began by explaining how Jesus had gone to Samaria, a place where most religious Jews refused to go. She compared it to the back streets of Toronto. Then she went on to read the portion of scripture she felt pertained most to the heavily made-up and scantily clad girls before her.

"When a Samaritan woman came to draw water, Jesus said to her, 'Will you give me a drink?' (His disciples had gone into the town to buy food.) The Samaritan woman said to him, 'You are a Jew and I am a Samaritan woman. How can you ask me for a drink?' (For Jews do not associate with Samaritans.)

"Jesus answered her, 'If you knew the gift of God and who it is that asks you for a drink, you would have asked him and he would have given you living water.'

"'Sir,' the woman said, 'you have nothing to draw with and the well is deep. Where can you get this living water? Are you greater than our father Jacob, who gave us the well and drank from it himself, as did also his sons and his flocks and herds?'

"Jesus answered, 'Everyone who drinks this water will be thirsty again, but whoever drinks the water I give him will never thirst. Indeed, the water I give him will become in him a spring of water welling up to eternal life.'

"The woman said to him, 'Sir, give me this water so that I won't get thirsty and have to keep coming here to draw water.'

"He told her, 'Go, call you husband and come back.'

"'I have no husband,' she replied.

"Jesus said to her, 'You are right when you say you have no husband. The fact is, you have had five husbands, and the man you now have is not your husband. What you have just said is quite true.'

"'Sir,' the woman said, 'I can see that you are a prophet. Our fathers worshiped on this mountain, but you Jews claim that the place where we must worship is in Jerusalem.'

"Jesus declared, 'Believe me, woman, a time is coming when you will worship the Father neither on this mountain nor in Jerusalem. You Samaritans worship what you do not know; we worship what we do know, for salvation is from the Jews. Yet a time is coming and has now come when the true worshipers will worship the Father in spirit and truth, for they are the kind of worshipers the Father seeks. God is spirit, and his worshipers must worship in spirit and in truth.'

"The woman said, 'I know that Messiah' (called Christ) 'is coming. When he comes, he will explain everything to us.'

"Then Jesus declared, 'I who speak to you am he.'" Heather paused, allowing the passage to soak into the three girls' minds and hearts.

"Do you understand what this passage is telling you, Jenny?"

The girl nodded slowly, a frown wrinkling her beautiful clear skin.

"I remember the story a bit from Sunday school. Jesus wasn't supposed to talk to her because he was a Jew and she was a Samaritan, but also because she was a—loose woman."

"That's right. The Son of God revealed his identity to a woman who had a reputation for being equal to a prostitute from a race of people the Jews looked down on. That story blew me away the first time I read it. It was as though Jesus was saying that this woman had just as much value in his eyes as any other person of importance.

"If he hadn't taken the time to get to know her, the rest of the town might not have listened to his message. Her life changed so much in the two days he was there that they all wanted to come and hear him. The Bible says that many more became believers and it was because of her.

"Maybe that's what Jesus wants to do for you girls. He can free you, and I've already told you that if you need to get away from Danny, we can move you up to the halfway house. That's what it's there for."

The girls sat there, mulling over Heather's wise council, hope flickering in the blackness of hearts that had long thought the word was nothing more than a dream. Maybe there was a way to get free of the chains of street life, and the child with the face of an angel and form of perfection continued in her quest for that freedom.

* * *

Shorty was getting frustrated. She was running out of time and didn't want to face Andy with her failure. Why had she even agreed to do what he asked? Heather wasn't such a bad person. Shorty just wanted things to go back to the old way. She missed Hildy and Jimmy even though they had all begged her to join them. She snorted to herself. Halfway house, indeed. She was quite content where she was.

She looked once more at the crumpled note in her hand, checking the message yet another time. She threw a worried glance at the mission entrance and then over to Heather, who sat chatting with a small group of teen girls who were heavily made up and dressed for prostitution. The girls had come in to warm up and Heather had gone to them. That had been Heather's itinerary the whole weekend through. She went from person to person, giving of herself without rest. Even when her boyfriend, the cop, came in, she continued to work with the homeless, the handsome man working alongside her.

A pang of guilt pierced Shorty, and she stared at the paper again. Heaving a sigh, she rose unsteadily and tottered over to Heather. Not giving her a chance to answer, Shorty stuffed the paper into the young lady's gesturing hand and then continued her trek to the mission door.

Heather excused herself instantly upon reading the scratchy writing on the paper and headed for the same door Shorty had exited only moments before. The snow had settled deep and heavy and she regretted not grabbing a coat to fight off the brisk wind. Following the small tracks, she detoured around a group of vagrants standing on the sidewalk and made her way through the alley that ran the length of the mission building to the empty lot behind it.

The tracks continued far down the narrow road that led behind the block of buildings. The air was cold and still and no one was about. Heather tramped through the thick snow, shivering every so often and wishing for that coat to cover her heavy sweater.

She spotted Shorty standing in the distance, her small dog shivering beside her, and was about to call out to the old woman when a hand clamped over her mouth from behind. Heather struggled like a wildcat, but the subtle fumes stinging her nostrils took their toll and she finally fell limp.

"Man, she's a fighter. Get her into the car. Andy will be pleased."

"What do we do with the old bat, Damon?"

"What did Andy tell you?'

"He said 'no witnesses.'"

"So, do what he says, idiot."

And no witnesses were left to see Heather stuffed, like a sack of feed, into a black car. No one remained to witness the car pulling out of the alley, carrying its unwilling cargo to another part of the city. No one but a scraggly brown mutt who sat, snarling and barking noisily beside his mistress' lifeless and bloodied body.

Twelve

HEATHER COULD FEEL THE EXCITEMENT rising in the room. This was a celebration like none other. At least it was for her. She breathed in the warm spicy smells of the steamed pudding as it sat in its metal cooker on the stove. The scent of roast turkey, dressing and potatoes mingled with all the other fragrances that come with a Thanksgiving dinner, and everyone was eager to feast on the bounty prepared.

But they were waiting. Two more guests needed to join the celebration and no one would dare start without them. She had listened diligently to the weather earlier that morning and was immensely relieved to hear that no snow was forecast for the weekend. They had already had a blast a week earlier, giving her small fits of anxiety until it melted, leaving the roads clear and dry.

Heather stole a glance toward Hildy and Jimmy snuggled side by side on the plump sofa. They were watching her, eyes twinkling with their own eagerness. Her eyes darted to her parents, brother, and sister, and each, in turn, regarded her with anticipation. She scanned the room, noting that all the residents were doing the same thing as she—looking and fidgeting.

Conversation was sparse. It would start, struggle painfully, and then fade. No one really cared to speak. They were too eager. They were waiting.

Chapter Twelve...

Deliverance Comes

"WHAT DID YOU DO WITH THE OLD WOMAN?" Heather could hear a familiar voice vaguely. Her mind swirled in a thick haze of narcotic and she felt gentle hands lifting her carefully from the back seat of the limousine.

"Her stupid mutt started yapping when we grabbed her. It bit my ankle and then started yapping. I had to move fast so no one would see us. I slit her throat and left her there. No one knows anything, and if they find the hag, they'll just think it was a street fight. We took your cash and left her. I didn't have a choice."

"Don't worry about it, Damon. You did your best. I have what I want."

Heather heard the brief conversation through a hollow tunnel and then she was gone again.

* * *

She awoke to an eerily familiar scene. The room was dark, all but the flickering of candles. She could hear the chants again. Almost the same song, she was certain. Her vision cleared and she could distinguish the hooded figures standing around her. Andy was there, hovering, waiting. He wore the dark cape she had seen in her dream and her heart leapt in sudden fear.

She awoke fully and realized that she was, like that first day with Andy those many years earlier, bound, and unable to move—this time strapped to a table. No. An altar. Fortunately, she was still clothed—an oversight on Andy's part, she was sure.

She quickly scanned the room, searching for the evil creature of her dreams, and, upon not seeing it, relaxed a fraction. Her stare returned to a different Andy. He was bulkier, more casual, and dead inside. His thick, dark hair was gone, replaced by the hollow and gaunt stare of a black skull tattoo. She shuddered as a realization hit her. The monster of her dream wasn't beside Andy; it was Andy.

Heather didn't need to ask to know what was happening. She understood completely. She had rejected Andy and he had turned to the closest thing to her—the demon she had housed. A part of her wanted to weep with pity. But Andy didn't want pity. He never wanted anything but power. She understood that now and felt a twinge of fear.

"What's the matter, Heather? Regretting leaving me?" He leaned over her casually, resting his arm on the table by her head. His face was so close and Heather turned away, refusing to speak.

"That's how it is, is it? Well, we'll see. We're going to have a little ceremony to welcome you back into the family. It won't hurt, I promise. It'll feel good—real good."

She closed her eyes and shuddered, forcing her mind away from the moment to dwell on the strengthening bonds of true love with a God who cared for her enough to give His life for her. The chanting increased in fervour.

*   *   *

"Where's Heather?" Jane had been looking for her all afternoon and was growing uneasy with each passing moment. Each time she asked the question, she was met with a shrug or shake of the head. She wasn't a woman known to panic, so others became concerned when they noticed her agitated state.

Angus, Jane, Charlie and Cyrus gathered as many people as they could and began to spread out through the city, checking all her old familiar haunts. The police had been called, but standard policy was to wait twenty-four hours. In this weather, she'd be frozen. David was quickly called and, claiming a family emergency, turned off his regular beat and headed toward the mission on foot.

It didn't take long for someone to discover Shorty, her throat slit, stuffed behind a dumpster in the parking lot behind the mission, and the police were called again, this time from the radio of one officer David Zavitz. Jimmy and Hildy were contacted with the fervent plea to pray, and the battle within the Heavenly realms escalated in its intensity.

The believers in the mission were quickly organized into groups, allowing them to pray around the clock, but no one had any desire to sleep. Those who had handed off the prayer chain found themselves gathering into impromptu groups in the common room to take up the spiritual fight in their own small prayer circles.

Shorty's body was carefully photographed and documented, then bundled up into the back of a newly arrived ambulance to be hauled off to the morgue for inspection. The small footprints of a mongrel dog were dutifully noted and then ignored, no one paying much attention to the direction in which they headed.

* * *

Heather didn't know how long she had been unconscious, but she did remember the cloying odour of the cloth as it covered her nose and mouth once more. Her tongue felt dry and stuck to the roof of her mouth. She sat up slowly, her head swimming in the drug's after-effects, and tried to look around her. Complete blackness enveloped her in a smothering blanket and she felt the panic rising.

Reaching out, she blindly felt her way, crawling, to the perimeter of her small prison and discovered she was in a box of sorts. It was made of wood and she could stand in it, take maybe four short steps each way, and lay down. Small holes were drilled in the top, allowing an occasional waft of air into the confined space. She sat again, taking stock of her person and surroundings. Her clothing still covered her, even her boots and coat. Nothing had been removed and she wrinkled her forehead curiously at that. Her wrists were chafed again, but only mildly. Her biggest concern was her thirst, and she leaned back against the wall and tried to think of other things.

What would her family be doing? Did they know she was missing? She had no idea how long she'd been gone but figured they probably did know by now. David would be frantic. Her mind followed another direction and she grew sad. Andy would never let Shorty out of that alley alive. Why did she do it? Heather couldn't comprehend the old woman's willingness to betray her when they had all tried so hard to include her in their new life.

An hour passed, allowing Heather time to assess her existence and how it had changed. Somehow, she couldn't feel the fear that she should. She remembered her dream of two nights before and shivered at its similarity to reality. She remembered the voice that claimed her as its own and smiled.

A song began floating through her mind, one of praise and rejoicing, and she hummed the tune, ignoring her dry throat as it interfered with the sweet sound of the haunting melody. And then the words came, soothing and faith-filled as she lifted them to the darkness and the voice.

"I hold such great assurance
within the tempter's snare
Because I know I'm hidden
within the Father's care,
And though the storms of life may come
and hold me in their clasp
I know that Christ's redeeming power
will comfort to the last."

Over and over, the ancient hymn rolled on the air, piercing the dark corners of eternity, flaunting the Redeeming power of the Blood of Jesus to all who opposed the Creator and the children He called His own.

Heather's heart swelled with a love and peace from beyond her and she closed her eyes, offering herself over and over in the words of the song. In the distance, she heard the slamming of a door and the loud clapping of brisk footfalls on tile as they drew closer. She smiled at the cloying darkness and renewed her song, tossing it to the air with the vigour and defiance of the reborn.

"So what's the cause for celebration?" The voice was heavily laced with sarcasm, but she knew it well, even through the muffling barrier of the wooden crate. Heather's silence answered Andy and he grew impatient. She heard the bolt scrape against its casing as he drew it back and opened the door.

At some point, he had flipped a light switch, flooding the room with bright light and rendering her eyes useless for a number of moments.

"Here. I thought you might like something to eat." Heather blinked rapidly as she tried to adjust to the brightness. She turned her head in the direction of the rattling of dishes and through a blur, saw the bottle of water. She lunged for it, ignoring the rest of the food. And then she stopped, remembering her first drink with Andy, and set it back down. He chuckled, remembering also.

"What? Don't you trust me? Here, I'll take a drink first, ok?" He popped open the bottle and took a small swig, handing the rest to his wary captive. Heather cast one last suspicious glance his way and then guzzled the cool refreshment until it was gone.

"I didn't know you were so thirsty or I would have brought more." Turning, he spoke to someone beyond Heather's vision, requesting another couple of bottles of water.

"So, Heather. What do we do now?" He leaned against the doorjamb and tried to act casual, but she could see the hunger and lust for power in him, struggling to gain control, struggling to consume her. She shrugged an answer and turned her attention to the sandwich before her, picking it up and nibbling daintily.

"It appears that whatever has taken over your life won't let me near you. And believe me, I've tried. I couldn't even touch your clothes without my spirit guide screaming at me. I tried that, too." He leered at her then, sending a shiver of apprehension down her spine, and she turned her back on him.

"Come on, Heather. Was life with me that bad? I loved you. I looked after you. What could you possibly have now that I didn't give you before? Maybe your cop boyfriend won't like you anymore when he finds out some of the stuff we used to do together." His dead smile turned into a sneer again and he nodded with satisfaction at her worried response.

"Yes, I do know about your man. I wasn't good enough, huh? Well, we'll see tonight. We're going to try again to introduce you back to your friend from the past and then you and I can have fun like we used to."

Heather shuddered at the memories and turned to face Andy fully.

"Do you honestly think that I would go back to that thing willingly? It was destroying me, eating me bit by bit. I'm free of it because Jesus is so much stronger. He forgave me and loved me. He can do that for you, Andy. Trust me, you don't want any part of that monster you call a spirit guide. It's a demon, not a guide, and it wants to destroy your soul. Get away from it while you can, Andy."

Andy threw his head back and laughed, insanity edging the chilling sound, and then an unearthly hatred shone through the husk that was all that was left of the man. Heather felt her hope drain away and resigned herself to the fact that her old captor was now captive to the very one who had held her for so many years.

She lowered her head then, offering a plea to her heavenly Father, praising Him for her freedom, asking for His protection. When she again lifted her head, Andy was gone and she was in darkness once more.

* * *

Jane began to cry when Shorty's note was found tucked into the collar of her nearly frozen dog. The older woman had found it in the snow after Heather had been snatched. It was spattered with fine drops of blood and crushed into a tight wad. She had done what she could with her last moments, jamming it under Whip's ratty collar while her life's blood pumped from the wicked gash in her neck.

Upon closer inspection, they discovered it had been printed on the back of stationary they knew all too well. Embossed on the bottom of the sheet was the title The Cully Club, and Cyrus cringed at what he now knew.

He stood there, slip in hand, looking from Jane, head bowed and weeping, to the crowds of street people milling around in the common room, to the front door. Years of street living had given him the ability to improvise quickly, solving the daily problems of survival. But now he was completely stumped.

He yearned to stay within the borders of the law because his Bible clearly outlined that he should do so unless it compromised

God's commands. He was in a quandary. Heather needed help. He knew where she was. By the time the police got the note, listened to the story of a scruffy old man, got a warrant, and actually went looking, she could be dead.

He dropped his gaze to the wiry-haired mutt huddled by his feet shivering. Bending slowly, and groaning at the inconvenience of aging, he scooped the small animal up and pulled him close, a tear welling in faded eyes. He dropped his forehead onto the rough neck and the dog turned and licked at his beard. And then he heard the tired voice of a man he knew he could trust and he straightened, heading toward him quickly.

David had settled himself heavily in a chair near the coffee pot to rest and warm himself. His lips were chapped from the wind and he was bone tired. Hopelessness threatened to consume him as he fought against one absurd idea after another. Maybe she got cold feet. Maybe she was afraid of marriage. Maybe she didn't really love him. Maybe Shorty wasn't the only one dead. He shook his head as though to chase the foul thoughts away, and for the hundredth time that day, lifted his plea to God, asking, begging for Heather's safe return.

Dropping his gaze to the floor, he never heard the silent approach of the old man and was startled when Cyrus finally cleared his throat gently.

"We just found this in Whip's collar. You remember Shorty's dog? She musta stuffed it there. It's written on paper from Heather's ex-boyfriend's club. We think he's got her, David."

The officer leaned forward and eagerly snatched the weathered paper from wrinkled arthritic hands. He scanned the page and frowned at its contents.

"Heather,

I been listening to the stuff you all have been talking about and I want to know more. Don't tell anyone 'cause I'm a bit shy about it. I'll wait for you in the back alley by the dumpster.

Shorty.'"

David's hand shook as he carefully set the letter down and snatched his radio from his hip.

"Don, get in here, we got a note. We know where Heather is."

* * *

"I don't care if we need a search warrant! She's there and needs our help now!"

David was almost yelling at his partner, so great was his frustration, and he raked both hands through messy hair for the third time since he'd contacted his partner.

"Dave, you don't know for certain she's there. It's been years since they had anything to do with one another and that old woman could have found the paper in a garbage can. For all you know, she could have had her throat cut for messing with some other street bum's dumpster. It's happened before."

The older, rotund policeman settled himself in a chair by the heater which ran the length of the common room and tipped it back to balance on two legs. He'd placed a call to the powers that be, requesting a warrant to search the apartment and club of Andrew Cully, recently released on parole. In view of his record and past interaction with David's fiancé, it likely wouldn't take long, but if they didn't wait and they barged in, the man could walk away and they might never find Heather.

David began pacing and muttering to himself, anger threatening to take hold and spill over until Angus approached, placing a gentle hand on his future son-in-law's shoulder.

"I know this is hard on you, lad, but the best thing that you could do for Heather is pray. Do you think that her Father in Heaven is unaware of the situation? Do you think that by fuming and ranting you're going to be of some service? Come sit, join me in prayer. If nothing else, you'll make an old man feel better about the disappearance of his daughter."

David hung his head sheepishly, feeling foolish over his tirade and lack of faith. How many times in the past had he done the very thing Angus suggested? He had been praying over Heather since he first laid eyes on her at fourteen. Why should this be any different? He nodded and allowed the Pastor to lead him to the table where his partner sat. The two settled across from Don and Angus turned his attention to the second officer.

"Sir, would you care to join us in prayer over Heather? We feel that it would likely be the most appropriate thing to do at present."

David's partner raised an eyebrow skeptically and shrugged, lowering the front of his chair back to the floor.

"Well, Reverend, it's like this. I'm not much of a man for religion. I've seen far too much hypocrisy and nonsense from people who call themselves Christians. My sister and her husband spend more time at church functions than they do with each other and can't figure out why they're having marriage problems. She goes to her women's coffee hours; he goes to his men's breakfasts. I give them a year before they split. Their kids are little hellions because they are so busy with their church things and then they have the nerve to call me a sinner and say I need to go to church. At least me and my wife are together and sticking it out. But all of that aside, I'll sit and listen, and if it'll calm Mr. "Antsy Pants" here, I'll even say a word or two."

Angus nodded gratefully and David looked at his partner oddly, surprised by his willingness to participate. Angus and David bowed their heads and closed their eyes. Don stayed as he was, a frown scuttling across his brow, and Angus began.

"Dear Father, you know what it's like to lose a child. Your own son left the perfection of Heaven, sacrificing himself for the sake of our lost souls. Oh how that must have tore at your heart. Now, Lord, I have once again lost my daughter, Heather, and my heart aches, too. I have so enjoyed the short time you have granted me with her and I would love to see it continue, but you have your reasons for everything and in this, I trust you.

"If Heather is to be returned to us safely, you have my gratitude, but if she is not," David gasped a harsh breath, "then give us the strength and peace to trust your decision to be the right one. I ask you to bring her home and I know you are able to, but I want what is best for your kingdom. If someone is going to be saved because of her sacrifice, then I know Heather would be overjoyed and I beg that you help us to understand. Lord, we place her completely in your hands. In Jesus' name."

David cleared his throat, trying to hold back the emotion, and took his turn.

"God, I'm such a fool. All this time, I've trusted Heather to you blindly. And then the one time where I should be placing her in your hands, I try to take over, thinking I can do it all better. Please forgive me for my selfishness and impatience. Help me to trust you no matter what happens. Lord, Angus is right. If someone is going to come to faith through this, then so be it and help me to be gracious. We know Heather loves you and that she'll be in Heaven waiting for us if something happens. Just help us to endure and to trust you. Thank you for her and for all you are doing to further your kingdom. In Jesus' name."

The silence stretched out as the two men waited patiently for Don to take his turn. Feeling awkward, he finally closed his eyes and started talking.

"God, if you're there, you know what I think of this religious stuff, so I'm not going to get real fancy here. I'm only doing this for my partner 'cause I care about him and want him to get his fiancé back. I don't have any reservations at all about asking you to bring her back safely. I'm not into any of this self-sacrificing stuff. Just bring her back, if you really are there and you even care. Oh…and help us get the warrant fast…and if she is with this scumbag, keep her safe. Amen."

Don opened his eyes immediately and cleared his throat, trying to act as if the whole prayer was no big deal. David looked directly at his partner, gratitude pouring from him as he reached over and punched the older man's shoulder.

"You are a true friend, man. Thanks for that."

* * *

The conversation continued between the pastor and the officers as they sat soaking in the heat and the coffee, waiting patiently for the call that would tell them the warrant was ready. No one noticed as Cyrus slipped away, carrying Shorty's small pet with him.

* * *

Heather didn't remember when she had fallen asleep, but the familiar sound of the lock startled her awake. She was thirsty again but had refused to drink, knowing that this time a drug would be present. Andy needed her will out of the way, but he didn't realize that Jesus would never give up her soul anyway.

Andy stood in the doorway while Damon took her gently by the arm, helping her to her feet as she looked at him questioningly.

"You don't seem to have a problem touching me. How come Andy can't?"

The goad hit its mark and Damon threw a worried glance at his boss. Andy's snide grin tightened and he stepped back, allowing his henchman to usher the young woman out of the crate that had been her home for two days.

"I have to use the bathroom." Heather threw a challenging look at Andy and he merely shrugged and nodded, following her right into the bathroom. She stopped inside the door and crossed her arms, cocking a hip in a gesture of defiance.

"If you think you're following me into the stall, you're in for a surprise."

Her captor leaned against the restroom door, willing to wait while she turned and entered the stall. Heather had to think quickly. With Andy not more than five feet away, there was no hope of climbing through the small window on the far wall. And then she grinned slyly as she remembered the T-shirt David had bought her earlier that year that read "WWJD—What Would Jesus Do?"

Quickly, she removed her jacket, hanging it on the door, followed by her sweater and the T-shirt. Smoothly, she slipped back into the turtleneck sweater, leaving her T-shirt on the hook of the stall door.

"What are you doing in there?" Suspicion and impatience mingled in the masculine voice, and Andy pushed off from the door, prepared to investigate. Heather was quick with her reply and proceeded with her use of the facilities.

"I just needed to take my coat off…if you don't mind?"

Andy peered at her thoroughly when she reappeared; checking to make certain everything was as it should be. He watched her carefully as she washed her hands and dried them with much deliberation. He still couldn't believe his luck in finding her again, and his mouth almost watered in anticipation of their reunion.

* * *

David divided his time between calling up Bible verses and praying. Don had leaned his chair back against the wall again to catch a few winks, and Angus had gone off to see to his family's needs. Headquarters had told them to stay with the family until further notice, but David knew it was more a case of keeping him from doing something stupid and rash.

The call came in with a loud squawk on Don's radio, waking him and bringing David to his feet. After a brief conversation, both men were heading out the door, eager to pick up their warrant and begin the slow turning of the wheels of justice.

The guard showed little resistance when the officers arrived, warrant in hand and, even offered to give them a guided tour of the office buildings and the club. The afternoon was fading into evening by the time the police finished inspecting each nook and cranny, and David was about to admit defeat when his partner reminded him that they hadn't been to the apartment yet.

* * *

Angus, Jane, Charlie, and Fiona gathered around the kitchen table in the small apartment they knew as home. Each pleaded with the God of creation, asking for intervention and protection. Each handed Him their faults and weaknesses and, in turn, clung to the grace and peace offered. Each boldly stood before him, reminding him of promises made through his word. And each prayed for the deliverance of their loved one and sister in Christ.

* * *

Heather followed the exit stairs to the apartment's basement with a dignity that came from the confidence of her place in Christ's family. Andy and Damon flanked her, the former keeping his distance, the latter holding her arm with a firm grip. Two other men followed, unknown by her. Each step brought her closer to the thing she feared the most—a test of her faith—but she was determined to keep that worry hidden from her captors.

She lifted her chin stubbornly and stared at the sign that hung on the dirty and paint-peeled door. "Basement." It may as well have read "Dungeon," so dark and dismal was its appearance.

Andy opened the door for her, allowing his cohort to usher her into the dim room. It was a large abysmal place. All the walls were painted black. If there were any windows, Heather couldn't tell and assumed they would be blocked in. A large door at the far end gave indication that, at one time, the vast room had been used as a parking garage, but she knew it had been closed off for years. Andy had purchased an adjoining lot and paved it for his tenants' use, rendering the parking garage off-limits.

Boxes and crates were stacked in piles throughout the echoing cavern, absorbing only a small portion of the hollow clicking of their heels as they made their way to the block wall opposite the door, stopping when they reached it. Surprise registered on Heather's face when Andy pushed on a brick and a section of the wall opened in, allowing them to enter a hidden room. She saw the pride on Andy's face as he watched her reaction and she turned away, placing her feet carefully in the growing darkness.

The door closed again, sealing shut with an echoing thump, and she jumped at the finality of the sound. Andy gestured her forward once more and she shivered, feeling the clinging tentacles of something innately evil hovering in the room ahead. Black and white striped candles flickered around the room, hung high in cast iron sconces.

A chandelier, hanging majestically from the ceiling, blazed with the light of dozens of candles, its beauty a dark and medieval thing. Beneath it rested the altar, that hideous stone and wood structure of death, its smooth surface smeared with a black, crusty paint. As she drew closer, it came to her that it wasn't paint and Heather felt faint with the realization that the altar surface was coated with old blood.

* * *

Cyrus had been right. Drawing on his decades of knowledge of the streets, he had easily found Andy's apartment building. What had made him go there first, he wasn't sure. Again, he felt the doubts surface as voices called distantly through his mind telling him to go to the club. No. He shook his head and prayed one last time for reassurance. Drawing a breath, he ducked around the corner of the building to make certain no one had seen him, and smiled as he caught sight of Andy's car, parked in its reserved spot. Thank you, Jesus. Where Andy was—that's where Heather would be.

It hadn't been easy getting the information he needed. He had been off the streets long enough to lose some of his contacts, and the ones he still had weren't very trustworthy. But he had managed.

Pulling himself back against the wall, he nonchalantly began his beggar's walk along the side of the complex, mumbling to himself as he swaggered along. To a passerby, he was merely another vagrant—a drunk—looking for a place to rest his head for the night.

The temperature was dropping fast as the evening was approaching and he worried that he might not find what he was looking for before it got too dark or too cold. Turning another corner, he spied it and breathed a sigh of relief. Billy had said he had to find the bush first, and there it was, fighting its way persistently between the crack in the pavement.

The shrub was scraggly and bare, hibernating from the bitter weather, but it was large enough to conceal the plywood-covered window behind it, and unless a person knew what to look for, the hidden entrance would remain hidden.

Looking nervously about him, Cyrus squatted down on his haunches and squirmed in behind the sprawling mass, pulling the small pry bar from its nest in the lining of his ratty, borrowed coat. Watching about him carefully, the old man slipped the end beneath the edge of the wood and leaned into the lever, prying the cover off after several tries.

No one saw him quietly pull the broken shards of glass from the window frame, nor did they see the black hole swallow the old man. And when he eased the wooden cover back into place, it was as though nothing had changed.

He dropped heavily to the floor, feeling the pain of the impact as old joints worked to cushion the fall. The room was dark and filled with tall stacks of boxes. Cyrus glanced around and limped his way to the nearest pillar of cardboard, melting against it for shelter. To his right was the old garage door, sealed shut with a line of rivets and caulking. Ahead was the exit door, leading to the apartments above. Boxes and crates were piled haphazardly all through the large underground room, creating a maze of sorts, and the old man didn't know where to begin.

He seated himself awkwardly on the floor, his back resting against a large crate, giving him time to think. Where would Andy hide her? Where would he put Heather where no one would find her? He was just about to pull himself to his feet and start a random search of the larger crates and boxes when he heard the distant exit door open and a familiar voice echo through the room.

"After you, my dear."

Cyrus clapped a hand over his mouth to keep the gasp from giving away his place of concealment, and silently thanked his Father for answering his prayers. Peering from the dim hiding spot, he watched as Heather, Andy, Damon, and two other ruffians worked their way through the aisles of debris to the wall not twenty feet to his left. He gaped in amazement as Andy pushed on a brick and Cyrus quickly counted—ten down from the ceiling, eight across from the stack of boxes—as the wall silently glided inward on an unseen track. And then they were gone, leaving the grizzled senior to question if they had even been there.

*   *   *

No one responded to the buzzer as Don rang it once more. David glanced impatiently down the street, hoping to see some way into the apartment complex. Andy wasn't answering the call button, and yet his car was parked in the reserved spot. After a moment's hesitation, the older officer picked a different button, grinning back at his partner when a feeble old woman's voice came over the speaker.

"Y-yes?"

"Madame, I'm a police officer and I need you to open the front door." Don frowned at the response.

"How do I know you aren't just some bad man wanting to rob me?" The voice crackled with age and uncertainty and he sighed impatiently.

"I'll tell you what. You call the police station. Ask if Officers Don Watkins and David Zavitz work there. If they say yes, let us in. If they say no…well…" He waited for a response.

"I think maybe I can trust you, but I'm not opening my apartment door unless you show some credentials." David smiled at the feistiness and took hold of the door handle, pulling the heavy door open at the sound of the buzzer.

"Thank you, ma'am." And they were in and moving stealthily along the halls, working their way up the stairs to the top floor where Andy's apartment was.

* * *

Heather shivered again and refused to take another step. There was no way she was laying on that horrid thing and she set her jaw, prepared to fight. Andy smiled at the stubborn set of her chin, recalling previous battles with an eagerness that got his blood pumping.

"Get on the table, Heather."

"No." She shook her head vehemently and crossed her arms. Andy looked past her and nodded, drawing her attention to the men who towered behind her. Damon grasped her in his powerful arms and she began to kick and struggle, adrenalin feeding her strength and making it difficult for him to hold her. Another man joined in, trying to get a grip on a flailing leg. He grunted as her boot connected with his ribs. Entering the fray, the third man grabbed the opposite ankle, holding tightly until his partner could catch his breath and continue with his own battle.

Leaning forward, she clamped her small white teeth onto Damon's exposed wrist, biting with all her energy, and he dropped her, pulling back with a bellow as he clamped a hand onto the torn flesh. Heather made her move, pulling the others off balance, jumping to her feet, and sprinting for the wall where the door had been earlier.

She was too slow. Andy had slipped around the struggling forms, planting himself firmly between her and the only exit the room offered. She skidded to a halt as he uncrossed his arms and spread them wide, knife glittering in the evil candlelight. With another nod of his head his men clamped onto her arms one more time. Careful to keep her at a distance, they half-dragged her to the corrupted altar.

She fought like a tiger, refusing to give an inch willingly, burning up more minutes as each man struggled to pin her to the table while cuffing her hands to the rings bolted onto the oak top. Damon grimaced as time and again Heather found places to sink her teeth. And then it was finished and they stepped back, furious with the vicious little cat.

Andy stood by, amused by the spirit and fight she had displayed, chuckling when it was over. Folding his knife, he tucked it back into his pocket and headed to the far side of the room. He picked up a cloth off of a shelf nearby and offered it to his assistant as the man put pressure on one bite mark after another. And then he went to stand by the woman he longed to possess and looked down on her hungrily, ignoring the heavy breathing of his attendants as they stepped back to allow him room.

The fight had gone out of her and she lay there quietly, as though nothing had happened. His smile wavered at her resolute strength and he turned to the wall hooks to don his cloak, nodding for the others to do the same.

In the struggle to subdue their victim, no one heard the soft whisper of the hidden door as it opened. The flicker of soft candlelight escaped their distracted notice as the gentle push of air stirred a small current in the room. And the slight scuffling of an aged body was left unheard by ears that were focused on the angry cries of the woman as restraint was forced upon her.

*   *   *

They found the shipping crate, complete with waste bucket, half-eaten food, and drained water bottles, on the ground floor of the building. It had been placed in an unused boardroom of some size behind the superintendent's office. The old man had put up quite a fight when the police opened his door and asked to see the office's contents, but threats of obstruction of justice soon quieted him. With the discovery of the makeshift prison, he clamped his mouth shut and sat with his arms crossed defiantly.

David was beside himself with worry as he began to search the floor, room by room. His faithful partner, after calling for backup, headed down one side of the hall while he took the other, and his heart almost burst when he heard Don's distant yell.

The spiritual battle for Heather's safe return spread to include the clerics as, one by one, they dropped by the MacDonald household. Soon the war moved into the living room as everyone found places to sit and continue to offer prayers of supplication on her behalf. Unseen by the mortal soldiers, the Heavenly realms shook with the struggle between the titanic forces of angel and demon.

* * *

Heather tipped her head back to watch as Andy, blackened by the concealing cloak, reached for a long, cloth-covered object. The others pushed themselves against the far wall, looking on hungrily as the sadistic man uncovered the long and wicked blade. It gleamed evilly in the candlelight, boasting with a silent voice of the lives it had consumed, and Andy drew a savouring breath through flared nostrils as though to smell the blood that had covered the knife earlier.

She looked on in a detached sort of way, observing from a distance and noting that it wasn't really a knife, but more like a short sword, curved and thick. Its grip was made of bronze and sparkled with stones like emeralds. Knowing Andy's love of ostentation, they probably were emeralds, Heather decided. She marvelled at her own calmness, wondering if she were merely asleep again, and dreaming. But no. It was real.

Again she turned her attention to Andy and watched sadly as he opened the book that held the evil curses and spells that called the demons and unspeakable creatures from the pit of Hell where they belonged. Her one regret was that she never got to say goodbye to her family. She never got to say "I love you" one last time to David. She sighed and forced her mind away from the spiritual stench of her surroundings, pulling her thoughts toward the light of her Saviour and the freedom He gave. The chanting began as Andy grasped both ends of the sword and raised it over his head.

*　　*　　*

The elevator sat empty and unused. Two officers stood guard to make sure of that. The aged superintendent had already been settled comfortably into the back of a police cruiser to await his fate.

David, Don and a small handful of others crept slowly and carefully down the exit stairs that led to the abandoned basement. David replayed over and over the feelings that came with the discovery of Heather's T-shirt on the back of the bathroom door. He wanted to shout with joy and then cry in fear. She had placed it there deliberately. And he knew it was her shirt. He'd given it to her.

No one made a sound as they slipped through the basement door into a blackened room. It was eerie and they could hear a strange humming sound in the distance. On the far wall light wavered dimly and the men moved toward it, unsure and cautious.

*　　*　　*

Andy's face was tight with concentration as he moved around the altar, chanting. His hand trailed along the table's edge, eager to touch, eager to own. He carried the dagger in his other hand, waiting for Heather's fear to mount enough that he could nick her and collect the blood drawn. But she wasn't afraid and he was growing frustrated. He threw an evil look at his companions and the three men chanted faster, raising their voices nervously.

*　　*　　*

Heather smiled, peace flooding her soul. Her true Master was with her and that was all that mattered. If she died, she knew she'd be with him and her heart almost yearned to be in his presence. She could sense the wall thinning that separated this world from the next. His presence swelled to an incredible intensity and then she began to sing again. From her mouth bubbled a song of praise and every inch of her being gloried in the presence of Christ as she felt his Holy Spirit join her in her worship.

* * *

"Shut up!" Andy couldn't believe his ears. She was singing. Her eyes were closed and she was singing about her God and his strength. He could feel the terror swelling in his chest at the horrible sound and he reached out and slapped her. Her eyes snapped open and she looked up at him with pity. He slapped her again and she began to sing louder.

His head began to throb as the beast he had called upon swelled with rage. How dare she defy him. He was too powerful. He wouldn't permit it.

Lifting his hands in the air, he all but screamed a prayer to the evil spirits that swirled below the surface of the atmosphere, thickening it with their rancid and corrupt presence.

"Spirits, I call on you now! Conquer the will of this, my bride! Consume her and overtake her! Break down those barriers that keep her from me! Fill her until she cries out with the overflowing darkness of your great powers! Trample her soul until it is under my command! Enslave her, bringing her into the submission of my will! I so command it!"

Closing his eyes, he renewed his chant, spittle flying from his lips and his voice hoarse. And then all was silent and he opened his eyes and looked down.

Heather lay there, a smile of beautiful purity spread across her peace-filled face, and Andy covered his ears and let out a wail as she began to sing again, worshipping her God from a heart set free through perfect sacrifice.

He'd had enough. He no longer wanted this piece of garbage. How could he have thought that she was even worthy of him? He would have ushered the spirit back in to her, bestowing amazing power upon her, but she had cast him aside. Things could have been as they were before she left, but with this new religion, she was worthless to him for anything other than a sacrifice. He slapped her once more for the pure pleasure it gave him, and drew the wicked instrument up high over his head, ready to strike.

The blade flashed in the flickering candlelight as it arced its way toward Heather's heart. Suddenly, Andy let out a loud yelp as he felt teeth sink into his ankle. He turned in surprise and looked down at a small brown dog that had leapt from the darkness and fastened its tiny, sharp teeth onto his lower leg. It's tenor rumble suddenly filled the hollow room as its anger grew. With a fierce kick, he sent the yowling animal into the trio of masked and hooded worshippers and continued his downward slash.

Metal met bone and flesh just as a loud crash sounded, startling the men trying to deal with the small bundle of fur and fury. Andy plunged the knife deep just as an officer yelled harshly at him.

"Freeze! Police!"

Ignoring the command, he withdrew the evil dagger and aimed again. A shot echoed through the room, silencing all activity, leaving only the heaving sobs of a young lady as she stared into the blank face of a grizzled old vagrant, who was stretched across her body, blood oozing from a knife wound in his back.

Andy gaped stupidly at his hand, raised for a second strike. Why wouldn't it move? He opened his mouth to speak, looking at Heather in longing. And then he fell; collapsing over the body he had just pulled the knife from. And he breathed no more.

* * *

David stood shaking as his stare went from the gun in his hand to the crumpled figures ahead of him. He watched in a daze as his partner rushed past, gun raised and ready, while yet another officer turned Andy onto his back. He was dead. Three other hooded and robed men stood to the side, hands raised, while more officers poured into the room. And then he saw her. Heather. Stretched out on the altar like some sacrificial lamb. A crumpled figure lay across her and David soon realized it was Cyrus as he quickly approached the hideous table.

They searched Andy, looking for the key to the chains that held her there and David barked once for his fellow police officers to be gentle as they lowered to the floor the broken and empty shell that was once the home of his good friend, Cyrus. And then Heather was free and struggling to rise. David wrapped his arms around her weak shoulders and lifted her from the bloodstained altar. She sobbed against him, gratefully allowing him to carry her from the dark place into sunlight.

* * *

Cyrus and Shorty were buried side by side, a contrast in life and in death, and a handful of people mourned over them. Heather held tightly to the small brown dog that had so faithfully stayed by Shorty. Why the dog had chosen to attack Andy, no one would ever know. She wiped a tear away, still unable to come to terms with Shorty's rejection of Christ and those who had decided to follow him. As for Cyrus, Heather owed him her life.

David stood close by as she placed a single yellow rose across each grave, contemplating the actions of her elderly friends. It would take a long time for her to understand what had driven the old man to leap between her and Andy's ceremonial knife. The image of his blank stare would stay with her forever.

And Andy was gone. Some thought she should be relieved, but she wasn't. She knew that the monster that had once owned her now owned him. She knew he would never be released from it. It broke her heart that he no longer had a chance to be redeemed as she had been, and that the evil one had claimed one more soul.

Wiping the tears that blurred her vision, she looked up to the headstone, placed with loving care by those who knew Cyrus so well. She smiled at the inscription they had all agreed on. Cyrus would be pleased. It was long but so appropriate. She read it one more time.

2 Timothy 4:7 and 8

"I have fought the good fight, I have finished the race, I have kept the faith. Now there is in store for me the crown of righteousness, which the Lord, the righteous Judge, will award to me on that day—and not only to me, but also to all who have longed for his appearing."

John 15:13
"Greater love has no one than this, that he lay down his life for his friends."

It is Finished

THE RUMBLE OF TWO MOTORCYCLES broke the silence in the room. Heather leapt to her feet, the unbearable wait over. A small, shaggy mutt jumped up with her, yapping in his high-pitched voice as he scampered ahead of her. She hurried to the front entrance, leaving the crowd sitting in their own anticipation. Throwing open the door, she stood, oblivious to the cold wind that whipped her auburn hair about her shoulders, and watched as two helmeted and bundled figures pulled up the snaking lane on their large, noisy machines. Whip hovered at Heather's ankles, small grumblings emanating from his broad and shaggy chest.

She watched as David dropped the kickstand and pulled his head from the protective casing of his motorcycle helmet, shivering at the biting air as he did so. He smiled at her, his own excitement surpassing the discomfort of the season's final bike tour, and then turned to watch another young man pull his own full-face helmet from his head, shaking his long dark hair loose.

His guest dismounted and stood uncertainly, eyeing Heather with a mixture of disbelief and growing excitement. He toyed absently with the dangling chinstraps and then the helmet was tossed aside as he opened his arms wide to welcome the young woman who hurtled toward him. They embraced while the others began to pour out of the log cabin, leaving its warmth for the greater purpose of watching the happy reunion. Whip stood on the step, whining his confusion as more attention focused on the pair.

Heather pulled back, tears streaming down her cheeks, and the young man lifted a gloved hand to wipe the dampness from the puckered scar.

"It's really you?"

Heather nodded mutely, marvelling at the face that was so identical to Charlie's. Her gaze skipped over the thick long black hair and the shadowed jaw to reach deeply into blue eyes that were so familiar and yet so alien to her. And then the smile split their faces as the truth took hold. Turning, the young man searched the assembled crowd, finding Angus, Jane, Charlie, and Fiona, and a look of joy crossed his face, filling his eyes with tears.

Heather watched as he silently sought forgiveness in the faces of those who stood around, and, once received, turned his perusal back to her, swiping at the dampness on his face with his sleeve. She tightened her hug, squeezing him with pent-up affection and reached up to kiss his rough cheek.

"Yes, George, it's me," she whispered to him, "and have I got a story to tell you."

Printed in the United States
95875LV00002B/91-138/A